Murder in the Wings
An Erica Duncan Mystery

By

Laura Shea

Copyright © 2020 by Laura Shea

For information, email Cozy Cat Press,

cozycatpress@aol.com or visit our website at:

www.cozycatpress.com

COZY CAT
P R E S S

ISBN: 978-1-952579-07-3

Printed in the United States of America

10 9 8 7 6 5 4 3 2 1

DEDICATION

To the Memory of Laureen Griffin, First Reader,
Always

ACKNOWLEDGEMENTS

I wish to thank Karen Galatz, my sister Sally Sweeney, and Deborah Williams for their kind and clear-eyed reading of my work. I hope you know how much this is appreciated. I also wish to thank Dr. Theodore Fields for his patient explanation of anaphylactic shock.

My sincerest gratitude to all!

Chapter 1

What we call the beginning is often the end. And to make an end is to make a beginning. The end is where we start from.
                              T.S. Eliot

The last of the boxes had been unloaded from the rental car. In late August, the two-hour drive to the lush greenery of Connecticut made a nice change from the baking sidewalks of Manhattan. As Erica Duncan took in her new surroundings, she noticed that the architecture of Canfield College tended toward the Gothic and the lawns toward the manicured. Silence filled the campus, which the undergraduates, still on their way, would soon end.

A college campus would normally be Erica's territory. It was Alan DeLorme, her significant other, who brought them to these leafy environs. She may have been the former English professor, but he was an actor enjoying the perks of a new celebrity. Alan had toiled on the stage for over two decades when a small role in a major motion picture brought him his first brush with real fame. The part he played was far from the lead, but it got him noticed. "A striking debut," announced the *New York Times*. "Who is this guy?" asked *Entertainment Weekly*.

Offers had been forthcoming, although nothing for the next three months, so Alan had accepted when the college came calling with a one-semester visiting position in the Theater Department. He would teach one course and coach the students applying to graduate programs on their audition pieces to be performed in the spring. By that time, Alan would have fled to the even greener pastures of the next acting job. For the time being, he would be paid significantly more than the typical assistant professor buckling under a four-course load. Alan's name and semi-famous face were already in the department's brochure and would attract students who had been promised the chance to work with *professionals*, including that guy they saw last week at the multiplex. The brochure failed to mention how short his tenure at the school would be.

Erica had come along for different reasons. She had recently departed an administrative position at a renowned Off-Broadway theater, where a co-worker had come to an unfortunate end by way of a blunt object to the back of her head. Undecided about what her next job should be, Erica was in no particular hurry to find out. She could spend the semester as Alan's plus one, but, with her own professional credits, she was more than qualified to teach a couple of sections of Introduction to Theater. When the department asked, she too said yes. She would be paid not at the superstar rate but as a lowly lecturer. Still, it would keep her out of trouble, and staying out of trouble was a job requirement that Alan had emphasized on the ride to the college.

"Do you think it's possible for you not to trip over a dead body while we're here?" he asked as they turned off Route 95.

"It's not like I go looking, Alan," she said.

"And yet they find you," he said with only a hint of sarcasm. "Maybe you could make yourself less findable. It's only for three months."

Erica knew what he meant. A trip to the country, to these luxuriant groves of academe, seemed just the thing. So would a few months without a murder.

"You act as if I do this deliberately."

"I'm not acting at all," Alan said. "No dead bodies. Not kidding, Erica."

"Actually, I'm here as the chief translator," she insisted. "We both know that academics speak a different language."

"But this is the *Theater* Department," Alan said. "I would think of them as a separate entity."

"I'm sure they do too," Erica agreed. "Separate and above, most likely. With their own set of norms and expectations. Hopefully, someone will pull you aside the first week and explain what they are. Over coffee or drinks, no doubt."

"I prefer the latter," said Alan.

"Good choice," Erica replied. "These little chats always go better with a drink in hand. But certain rules will apply. Some may seem odd or strange to you, like a language that does not fall trippingly off the tongue. That's where I come in. I'm fluent in their language."

"Understood," Alan said.

"And I have plenty to keep me busy," she continued. "Besides my teaching assignment, there will be all the meals I'm not cooking, so I'll need to scope out the local restaurants. We don't want to starve."

Alan looked bemused but managed to keep at least one eye on the road.

"The apartment does have a kitchen," he said.

"How nice," she replied. "And you are welcome to try it out. I, on the other hand, am intrigued by that quirky little theater they have on campus. The Brink. It has an interesting history. Close enough to New York to try out new shows, at least back in the day. Mostly in the summers when the students weren't around, so there was a stage that was empty and available. And far enough away to keep the critics at bay until they wanted them to visit. *The Provocateurs* started here, which went on to a long run pretty much everywhere on the planet. Too bad the college didn't co-produce that one. It certainly would have boosted the endowment. I have a feeling all they got out of it was the cost of the theater rental."

"We'll have to ask them," Alan replied in an even tone. "Maybe not the first day."

When they pulled up in front of faculty housing, Erica still felt the car's vibrations as she stepped onto solid ground. They began moving the boxes, assisted by the eager undergraduate assigned to help them, who referred to them as Professor DeLorme and Ms. Duncan, a slight error on their helper's part that she would soon rectify, though not while he was toting their possessions to the elevator and then to their temporary abode. Erica never caught his name but thought of him as Mercury, given the speed with which their move into faculty housing was completed. Tall and thin, he also appeared to be surprisingly strong. The boxes would be unpacked later, but that was outside Mercury's purview. With the mission accomplished, followed by their genuine thank you's, he left as quickly as he came.

"Nice of them to throw in a rent-free apartment," Erica said, as she looked around the tidy one bedroom that would be their home until the end of the semester.

"I wouldn't advertise that," Alan said. "I don't think that housing is free for the rest of the folks who live here."

"Or furnished," said Erica. "Where will it end?" she asked while surveying the well-worn sofa and chairs, the décor enhanced by the boxes that filled most of their living space.

"And if you think they don't know every detail of your contract, think again, my friend," she added. "'Confidential' has a whole different meaning around here. In fact, it pretty much doesn't exist. Someone will have told someone, who will have told someone else, and on we go."

"Also good to know," said Alan.

"It's nothing to worry about, really," Erica said. "Those in the know will be quietly pleased that they know. Information being power and all. Though they won't be too thrilled that you make more money, even in the short term."

"I wasn't worried, really," Alan replied.

"Think of it as your first lesson," said Erica. "With many more to come."

The ring of the landline interrupted their conversation. Once he located it, Alan quickly answered. On the other end, a female voice offered an effusive welcome, which Erica could hear from across the room.

"Alan, is that you?" she asked. "It's Cressida. McPheers. Chair of the Theater Department. I'm glad to hear that you're in the apartment."

"We made good time," Alan said. "And thank you for sending over the student to help us move in. I didn't catch his name."

"Student? Um, hmm. I didn't realize we had sent anyone." The line was quiet for a moment. "Someone must have thought of it and sent him over. We have a great staff here, always thinking ahead."

"Well, whoever it was, send him or her our thanks. From Erica and myself."

"Certainly," said Cressida. "And you've probably just pulled in, but would you and Erica join me for cocktails this evening? Very informal. Just a few members of the department. Before the undergraduates arrive and the onslaught begins."

A "yes" would seem to be required, so Alan gave Erica a quick look and answered in the affirmative.

"Of course, we'd love to come by for a drink," he said as Erica mouthed the word "Tonight?" Alan nodded. "Let me know what time and where," he continued.

"Wonderful!" Cressida said as she gave him an address and quickly explained how to get there, following her instructions with "It's within easy walking distance. So much is, around here. You'll see. Sevenish, if that works for you."

"Seven would be fine. Looking forward to it," said Alan, as the conversation ended and he put down the receiver.

"Word travels fast," Erica said. "She already knows we're here? I guess Mercury reported in."

"Not to her," said Alan. "She says she didn't send him. She wants us to come over for drinks and to meet a few members of the faculty. 'Very informal,' she insists."

"I hope there are 'eats' as well. We don't have time to do much more than clean our travel-stained selves. How long will it take to get there?"

"Not long at all, she assures me. Apparently, everything is within easy walking distance."

"Oh, goody," said Erica. "A very tight community. No doubt we'll be bumping into each other at the local market."

"Unlikely they'll be bumping into you," he said, smiling.

"Well, somewhere else then. If not the butcher, then the baker, the candlestick maker, wherever people congregate," Erica insisted.

"Tonight, it's the home of Cressida McPheers," Alan replied.

"Sort of makes one yearn for the general indifference of schools in the big city, and the far flung addresses of the people who teach there," sighed Erica.

"Well, I plan to return the rental car tomorrow morning, but there's always train service back to the city. If or as needed. In case you miss the noise, the crowds, the people."

"Not yet," said Erica. "I signed on for three months and two courses. In for a penny, in for a pound. Which is roughly what I'm getting paid for this gig."

"Hopefully, we can make up for that in perks."

"I hadn't heard about those," said Erica. "Do tell."

"I don't have time now," said Alan. "We can cover that later. Let's say, tonight, back here, after a couple of drinks at the party."

"Deal," said Erica. "I took a quick peek in the bedroom. It's a new mattress, still wrapped in plastic. Very thoughtful of the housing people. Can't wait to try it out."

"Why wait?" asked Alan.

"No time like the present," he said, with which Erica wholeheartedly agreed.

Chapter 2

I drink to make other people more interesting.
Ernest Hemingway

Cressida McPheers knew how to give directions, which certainly came in handy as the longtime chair of the Theater Department. Erica and Alan found themselves on her doorstep in less than ten minutes without having to resort to asking for more directions or adopting the speedy pace known as city walking. While Cressida's instructions were clear, sevenish had a different meaning once you crossed state lines. In New York, sevenish meant not a minute before seven and probably well after, unless you were part of the catering staff. Here it seemed to mean "first come, first served," and no one wanted to go home thirsty. Several of the partygoers looked as though they had arrived before Cressida issued her invitation to Alan and Erica. Perhaps it wasn't fair to judge these new colleagues by their alcohol intake. After all, summer vacation was not officially over, so no one was on duty or required to be on their best behavior. Still, Erica was a little taken aback by the general ambiance. As it turned out, theirs were not the only new faces in the room, so this would be the newcomers' welcome to the Theater Department, at least the Theater Department at play. Based on the available evidence, the department's motto would seem to be "Drink up."

The introductions to her colleagues had gone so quickly that Erica, even on her first glass of wine, had absorbed almost none of the names. Alan was clearly the draw here, which Erica fully expected. He had been taken over by a group, including their new boss, who wanted to hear what it was like to work with whomever on that play/film/episode of *Law and Order*, to be followed by a lively round of "Do You Know . . . ?" Alan had been around and had the stories to prove it. Erica's imagined advice to the group would be something along the lines of "*Down, boy (or girl). Best to take it slow. Don't want to run out of stories before midterms.*

Aware of the side eye she was receiving from a few people she had yet to meet, Erica felt that she was being inspected rather than welcomed to the department. Edging away from the crowd, she wondered if she would ever be able to sort out the ones who taught playwriting, directing, design, and, of course, acting, as well as the ones who acted in life or merely on the stage. Her own recent brush with the People's Theater would add cachet to her resume if she chose to mention it, but she had no particular desire to play that card. It would require a recap of how a Kemby award, theater's biggest prize, landed at the back of someone's skull in a case of murder that Erica had a hand in solving. Both hands, actually.

Retreating from the fray, she met a kindred spirit at the fringes of the room, looking as quietly surprised as she was. Tasha Cooper, an African American woman not yet out of her twenties, was a brand new assistant professor, having graduated from a dizzying array of elite institutions. Given her striking looks, Erica guessed that her field was acting and that she belonged on the stage. She quickly learned that Tasha's area of expertise was Balinese theater, two words that Erica had never put together. Tasha assured Erica that

Balinese theater had influenced the works of everyone from Antonin Artaud to William Butler Yeats.

"So, pretty much the whole alphabet," Erica said.

"Pretty much," said Tasha, smiling. Tasha would teach her area of expertise to the advanced undergraduates, but, she assured Erica, she was also assigned to teach the standard Ibsen/Strindberg/Chekhov/American authors course required of all majors, minors, or innocent bystanders with an interest in theater.

Before their conversation could get much further, Cressida McPheers had an announcement to make. Her ability to quiet a room was impressive. Although fulsome on the phone, she had perfected the technique of stopping the talk by not talking. Those standing closest to her took the cue and did the same. Silence spread quickly through a room that just seconds before had bristled with energetic conversation.

Cressida began by stating the obvious. "I have an announcement to make," she said.

As she did, Alan ambled back to stand near Erica, where a quick introduction to Tasha ensued. Erica then whispered to Alan, "Is this the part where she sits on the piano and sings 'I'm Still Here'?"

"Why are you asking me? This is your land," Alan countered, also *sotto voce*.

"These are your people," Erica said.

"Then I would guess, no," said Alan. "Too soon."

"Then I'll wait with bated breath," said Erica.

"Something tells me you won't have to wait that long."

Scanning the crowd, Cressida began. "Hello," she said. "Welcome back to one and all. I know we are all looking forward to the productive and creative year ahead of us."

Based on the look on their faces, those in attendance were split on that decision.

Regardless, Cressida persevered. "First, I want you to know that all theater students, and that includes everyone enrolled in any theater class, will be required to do a performance piece at some point during this semester. Performance art, as you know, can happen anywhere and take any form. It can integrate theater, art, or music and is often interdisciplinary. It can be spontaneous and unrehearsed or carefully scripted, both in word and action. Although the performance could well be available on video streaming, we are requiring that students be present for their performance piece, that it be done live. These performance pieces can happen anytime and anywhere, using any number of performers, for any amount of time."

The reactions of her listeners ranged from eager nods, from those who had helped to come up with this plan, to polite befuddlement. Erica landed somewhere in the middle, while Alan seemed to be withholding judgment. Cressida soldiered on.

"The key to performance art, as I don't need to tell you, is the relationship between the audience and the performer. As audience members, we may be called upon to become spectators or active participants, or spectators, then participants. In any case, we must not interrupt the performance, wherever it takes place, until it becomes clear what our role should be. With this clarity will come the certainty of how to proceed. And we want our students to have a memorable encounter, one they will never forget. I hope to experience many of these firsthand. Since they are unscheduled, I can't be at all of them. When you do come upon one of these performances, please make a note of the name of the student or students involved, and a brief description of what you saw. Our plan is to make this an annual event.

We hope to create a catalogue of the various types of performance art we experience, both as a guide and an inspiration for future generations of students."

Cressida was not quite finished. After a dramatic pause, she added, "and we have a mystery to solve."

Alan had listened politely until Cressida's mention of the word *mystery*. His demeanor quickly changed, and he stared at Erica, who could feel his look on the side of her face. If looks could kill, this one just might.

"It seems that there have been some ghostly sightings at the Brink," Cressida continued. "We have always had a ghost, the ghost of our dear benefactress, Rosaline Vander Brink, whose generosity built our theater. If not for her advanced thinking, our beloved Brink would not be. Especially rare for an upper class woman in the nineteenth century, when the entire acting profession was viewed as disreputable, and actresses in particular, equated with prostitutes. So-called respectable citizens would refuse to rent them a room or seat them at a table in their restaurant. But that was then and this is now. Now, of course, the most successful in the acting profession are viewed as royalty."

Cressida eyed the room to make sure her audience was still watching intently. Given that many of them would rely on her for their future employment, they were rapt.

"Now, our dear Rosaline is, of course, welcome in the theater she built and that we all share. Her presence has often been felt, especially at night, occasionally in the rustling of the curtains that frame our stage. There have been recent reports of doors being left unlocked and various items disappearing from the shelves or supply closets. This is not Rosaline's style at all. While our dear benefactress might occasionally have a little fun with us, we must all be watchful for anything out of the ordinary in or around the theater."

With a final pause, Cressida seemed to be finished. Her audience nodded in tacit agreement and returned to their previous conversations or made another trip to the makeshift bar on Cressida's dining room table. Erica was left wondering about what she had just heard. Was this a coded message to those in the room who might be leaving doors open to raid the supply closet, then put the blame on poor Rosaline? Stranger still, Cressida, like many in the room, seemed to take this ghostly presence for granted, a given in their daily lives, nothing out of the ordinary. Erica added their curious definition of *ordinary* to her lexicon, the type of ordinary that would soon include hundreds of students popping up at any moment to enact their very own piece of performance art, intended to dazzle and amaze. Erica had the feeling that they might be in for a long semester.

Alan's glare had subsided, but Erica could still sense his concern. She turned to him and whispered, "Not to worry. She said *mystery*, not murder. And dear Rosaline is already dead."

"Dead but not buried, apparently," Alan replied. "And still with the keys to the kingdom."

Chapter 3

Education is an admirable thing, but it is well to remember
from time to time that nothing worth knowing can be taught.
Oscar Wilde

A few days later, the semester began. Students in the
know refer to the first week of classes as "syllabus
week." With any luck, the faculty member will simply
review the syllabus on the first day of class, an activity
taking about twenty minutes, with no actual teaching
taking place. Best to ease in gently to this great
adventure. Most of the faculty agreed with this teaching
philosophy and complied. A few, Erica included, felt
that more of an effort should be put forth at the first
meeting, if only to show that the professor meant
business. To this end, she brought to class copies of a
short play by Susan Glaspell entitled "Trifles," inspired
by a case that Glaspell had covered as a journalist in the
early twentieth century, a story she would also turn into
a short story re-titled "A Jury of her Peers." All three
versions tell the story of a farm wife accused of killing
her husband as he slept. The fictional versions make use
of a noose tied around his neck as the murder weapon.
In the factual version, the woman was charged with
taking an ax and giving her husband several whacks to
his head, a kind of working class Lizzie Borden. Unlike
Lizzie, who could afford to hire a former governor of
Massachusetts as her defense attorney, the poor
farmer's wife lacked the funds for similar legal counsel,
and watched stoically as an all-male jury, on
circumstantial evidence, found her guilty.

While there had been some talk in town about the physical abuse suffered at the hands of her husband, not a whisper made it into the court record as part of her defense, for fear that it would sully the name of the deceased. In the court of public opinion, however, the evidence that weighed most heavily against the farm wife was her demeanor during the proceedings. While Miss Borden had cried and occasionally fainted during her trial, sure signs that she was truly a lady—a lady being incapable, either morally or physically, of committing murder—the farmer's wife held in her emotions during the trial and when the verdict was read. In real life, the guilty verdict and imprisonment were followed by a successful appeal, followed by the legal system choosing not to retry her. In the fictional version, the outcome is left open, as two women, a jury of her peers, decide what to do with evidence they discover in the kitchen of the accused.

In class, there had been no lack of volunteers to read the short play. Erica had to double and then triple up on parts to accommodate all the eager participants. She hoped that this was a sign of things to come. She feared that a few of them might be under the impression that they would be reading twelve-page plays all semester, although the list of required readings on the syllabus told them otherwise. Either way, day one had gone well. After a brief discussion, she decided to quit while she was ahead. Class dismissed.

Since Erica taught her two classes back to back, she had a short day, and decided to look for Alan to see if he wanted to take an early lunch. When the semester was in full swing, it was unlikely that this would be possible, at least on the teaching days they shared. She strolled over to the theater where Alan was assigned to teach his acting class, the stage being his classroom. Although she had never actually visited the theater,

Erica knew where to find it in a far corner of the administrative building in which it was housed. Her first clue was the hammering she heard from behind a door in the theater lobby. She opened it to find a set of stairs that led down to the shop. There, she encountered a flurry of activity in the form of scenery being built for the first production, which had yet to be officially announced. Alan's fame had preceded him. Since everyone seemed to know who he was, she could skip to the question of his whereabouts.

"I saw him onstage," said one student, who, unlike most of this crew, had heard her question but was far more interested in the flat he was painting. "Just follow those stairs back up. Turn right and they lead to the stage."

Erica followed his directions, and worked her way to the backstage area. The Brink had a small backstage, not large enough to accommodate a cast of thousands but sufficient for the number of actors needed for the plays performed at Canfield. These were female-centric whenever possible. The once "all-girl" school had gone coed decades earlier, but the male population still had a way to go to equal their number. Theater was where the girls were, so there were always male recruits only too happy to join this merry band if it meant meeting more of their female counterparts. For some, it was a chance to find like-minded individuals who shared a passion for the stage or for each other. Either way, the Theater Department could always use more of them.

The student had been confident in his directions. Unfortunately, he was wrong about Alan, who was nowhere to be seen. In fact, no one was in the theater, or so it first appeared to Erica. Seizing her chance to tread the boards, Erica walked across the stage that was lit by a single work light. Still, Erica could see out into the darkened theater, which held just under two-hundred seats, twelve rows downstairs and four in the balcony. Given the activity further downstairs, the theater was eerily quiet, the lonely blue light only enhancing the mood.

Erica continued her walk to the far side of the stage. With the exception of the work light, the stage itself, with the requisite brick wall at the back of the acting space, was bare. *The better to hear you with?* Erica wondered, since every proscenium stage seemed to be bordered by brick. In various corners, she could see coils of rope and cables or assorted lighting fixtures waiting to be hung and focused.

Erica had entered stage right, but it quickly became clear that there was no possibility of exiting stage left because there was no exit stage left. Instead of making their way to the dressing rooms when their scene ended, actors found themselves face to face with the brick wall that was stage left. There might be room for a single piece of lighting equipment but there was no exit. To avoid a lopsided blocking plan, actors had to be directed to enter and exit from that side of the stage. Unless the set designer took pity on them and built a set that included a passageway behind the action onstage, actors would have to wait until their next entrance and, when they had a chance, they could exit stage right.

Erica wondered why the theater had been constructed this way. From what she had seen, the college did not lack for funds. The general artsiness of the campus made Theater a popular major. Surprisingly, these students had not been hounded into more "practical" majors by parents expecting an immediate return on their hefty investment of tuition. Maybe their offspring hadn't shared the news of a sudden shift from economics to acting. (Graduation day might be a bit of a shock.) Maybe the parents didn't care, and for them, the tuition *was* a small price to pay.

Still, no renovations to the structure of the existing theater had been made. Was this a requirement of the otherwise forward-thinking Rosaline? Even a quick trip to the outdoors and a run behind the theater (sheltered by an awning at the very least) would be preferable to cooling one's heels stage left, with no room for a bench or even a chair.

Curious, Erica thought. Having seen enough, she was about to turn and go when she caught sight of a large coil of rope at the farthest corner of the stage—stage left, of course. On top of the rope, a small female lay, curled in what looked to be a slightly relaxed fetal position. Erica moved closer. Upon inspection the young woman appeared to be sleeping. Her pale white face was made paler by the camouflage of shoulder-length black hair fringed by a set of bluntly cut bangs. The expression on her face was peaceful, blissfully so, though she did not look to be taking deep breaths as she slept. Erica tried to wake the girl with a gentle nudge to the insole of one of her feet. It worked, which relieved Erica but angered the beautiful dreamer, who sat up with a start. Her angelic demeanor was quickly replaced by an anger that belied her previously tranquil expression.

"You ruined it!" the young woman cried, pronouncing the word as *runed*, as if she were describing a letter from an ancient alphabet.

"Your nap?" asked Erica, a little surprised by the level of irritation displayed by the student. "Not the comfiest place to sleep," she said. "Wouldn't you be happier back at the dorm?" *In a bed*, thought Erica, always a fan of creature comforts.

"Not my *nap*," replied the student in a tone suggesting that this should be obvious. "My performance piece," she insisted, regaining a small degree of calm. "I was hoping to see the ghost of

Rosaline when she visited the theater. When it was empty, of course. I was turning my waiting into a performance piece."

You're who that does what? thought Erica, who managed to say, "You know that there are all sorts of people downstairs. The stage may be empty, but the theater isn't."

"I *know*," the girl answered a little testily. "But they have to leave by a certain time, and when they lock the theater, I planned to hide so they would lock me in. So I could see her. Rosaline. And get an A on my performance piece at the same time. Which you ruined," she repeated, looking daggers at Erica, who chose not to mention that one person sleeping on a coil of rope did not an empty theater make. Not only that, but the performance was supposed to be experienced and noted by a faculty member in the Theater Department. If this student's plan was successful, then only the ghostly Rosaline would be in attendance. Unless Rosaline and Cressida were in regular contact, which Erica did not discount as a possibility, then the student would have some explaining to do in order to receive credit for her efforts.

Erica chose instead to underline the obvious.

"You do know it's nearly noon, not midnight," she said.

"*Yes!*" the student snapped.

"Okay," Erica said, stretching the word. "What were you going to call it?" she asked. "Your performance piece, I mean," Erica added when the student looked confused.

"Chimera at midnight," she replied, still miffed but recovering.

Pace, Orson Welles, thought Erica, but left it at "I'm sorry to have disturbed you. I didn't realize."

"Well, the mood is broken, so I'm leaving," the student sniffed, pulling herself up from the coil of rope that had been her resting place.

"So am I," said Erica, as the two quickly crossed the stage, moving in opposite directions when they passed through the theater's exit.

"Welcome to the Brink," said Erica to herself as she made her way home.

Chapter 4

All the world's a stage and most of us are desperately
unrehearsed.
Sean O'Casey

After class, Alan had been invited out to coffee with three of his students from the advanced acting class. It's usually another faculty member who pulls aside the new hire to give him or her the lay of the land. These three had taken it upon themselves to share with Alan their world view, at least in terms of what they saw as the most relevant information. This turned out to be about them and their standing in the department. As Alan cheerfully reported to Erica when they met later that afternoon in their still unpacked apartment, the three students, named Alexis, Ashley, and Ava, were the current queen bees, sharing equally between them the lead roles in all major theater productions.

"They refer to themselves as queen bees?" asked Erica, incredulously.

"They didn't have to," Alan said. "The message was clear."

"But you don't have anything to do with auditions or casting the productions," Erica began.

"I know," said Alan. "They seemed to know that too. It wasn't so much that they were trying to stack the deck in their favor. It was more of a 'this is how it is,' rather than 'this is how we would like it to be.' In their opinion, it is what it is."

"And what is it?" Erica asked.

"A done deal," said Alan. "It seems that Alexis Grinnell plays the lead in the serious dramatic production in the fall. Ashley Kwan gets the lead in the musical they do in early spring, and Ava Levitan finishes strong with the comedy at the end of the semester."

"Confident little darlings, aren't they?"

"They have reason to be. They have ruled the roost since they were sophomores and have no reason to think that anything will change."

"How did they manage that? Usually, there's an element of 'wait your turn' about these things. What did they do? Kill off the competition?"

Once the words were out of her mouth, Erica regretted them. To Alan, this was no joke.

"Whatever they did, however this came to be, it is none of my concern, your concern, our concern. The departmental politics will have to play out without us. My responsibility begins and ends with getting them ready for their auditions for graduate school."

"And these three will be favoring their audience with what rendition?" Erica wanted to know.

"That's easy enough," Alan answered. "Blanche, Blanche, and Blanche. Many rides on that *Streetcar Named Desire*. Different speeches but the same idea. I tried to suggest alternatives, since they will undoubtedly be competing for places at the same schools."

"They won't be the only three Blanches at the audition," said Erica.

"I'm sure you're right," Alan said. "They are very different and bring different skills to the table. Even from our first class meeting, that's clear. But their collective mind is made up. Blanche it is."

"I hope they're not relying too heavily on the kindness of strangers, especially the ones watching their eighteenth Blanche of the day," said Erica. "And what a shame that there are no good roles written for women since the middle of the twentieth century." She added a dramatic pause before exclaiming, "Wait a minute! Actually, I can think of one or two—"

"As I said, it's their call," Alan interrupted. "I'm here to provide audition advice."

"And what is your advice?" she asked.

"Learn your lines and don't bump into the furniture," Alan replied, "Always a good place to start."

"Then I wish them the best," Erica said. "So, break a leg. Or possibly three." She added, "And when will you three—I mean four—meet again?"

"Not soon," said Alan. "Everyone's getting revved up, I mean, prepared for the first round of auditions on campus."

"Oh, the one that the first one—"

"That would be Alexis," Alan said helpfully.

"Yes, her. And she will be playing the lead in . . . ?"

"*Hedda Gabler*, as it happens. If things move along as they fully expect it will, the world will be treated to her Hedda."

"So Eilert Lovberg's back in town. I guess we'll see if things play out as you say they will."

"I'm just the messenger," said Alan. "It's their message."

"Let's see if it gets through," Erica finished.

Chapter 5

Put out the light, and then put out the light.
William Shakespeare

The pop-up performances made their public debut.
At the lunchtime rush a few days later, an eager
sophomore regaled the cafeteria with his rendition of
the "To be or not to be" speech from *Hamlet*, when the
Danish prince debates the advantages of living versus
dying. Living ekes out a victory, just barely, due to the
fact that no one, including Hamlet, knows what happens
after death—no one has made it back to give us the
final word—so it's too scary to chance it on a trip to
"the undiscovered country," the great unknown. As a
result, whether prince or pauper, we put up with the
heavy lifting of life.

Although barely heard over the din, his message
managed to get through. The Psych majors took it as a
cry for help and immediately contacted the Counseling
Center. The English majors knew the speech and could
identify it as Shakespeare, while the Theater majors
knew bad acting when they saw it and agreed that he
was in need—of more rehearsal. The description of his
performance travelled so far and so fast that by the time
her students reported back to Erica, it was old news. It
seemed that no faculty member had actually been in
attendance—few braved the cafeteria at lunchtime,
taking their midday meal anywhere but there. The
performance was so widely discussed, however, that
many felt as if they had been there—or said that they
had—and the student passed the assignment, which was

all the Finance major wanted. Unfortunately, the easy A he expected from Introduction to Theater would not, in the end, be forthcoming.

Across the campus, another scene was playing out, to a much smaller audience. On the stage, hours earlier, students had lined up to audition for *Hedda Gabler*, even though most believed that the title role was already cast. One student had stayed behind, resting by a coil of rope in a far corner, seeming not to breathe. This was probably due to the fact that her heart had stopped. If she could have called out, it would have made no difference. The set crew had put away their hammers and paint brushes, leaving no one in the theater as she had planned, still hopeful of meeting the ghostly Rosaline on one of her nightly visits. No one would have heard or could have helped her, given the suddenness of her demise. If Rosaline had been in the house, she kept herself to herself.

When the dreadful news was confirmed, an all-points bulletin went out via text to the theater faculty, including two of its newest members. Erica was seated at the kitchen table, wondering why Formica had ever gone out of style. The table was covered by the take out menus she had collected during the first weeks at Canfield. Alan looked at his phone, then at her, and this time, it was his turn to look stunned.

"What is it?" Erica asked, reading his expression.

"A female student has been found, dead, in the theater," he began. "She was on the stage, on top of some ropes. No signs of foul play, cause of death to be determined."

More may have been coming, but Erica quickly interrupted.

"Oh, God, no," she said, pushing away the menus in front of her.

"It's shocking, yes, but at least you were nowhere near it."

"Well, actually—" Erica began.

"You were here with me," Alan insisted.

"Of course, I was," said Erica. "Our alibis are firmly in place."

Seeing his evident distress, she waited a moment before adding, "There's no need to jump to any conclusions. There could be a completely innocent explanation. It could have been an undiagnosed condition, or some health problem she knew about. It would still be tragic, but nothing requiring alibis."

Alan looked again at his phone while answering, "Maybe you're right." Then quickly shifting gears, he added, "It says she was a sophomore. What does that make her? Eighteen? Nineteen? Eighteen to nineteen year olds don't just die."

"Sometimes they do," replied Erica. "And I know you don't want to hear this, but on the first day of class, I did see a student sleeping on a coil of rope in a corner of the stage. I went looking for you after class and found her instead. She planned to stay in the theater, alone, in hopes of communing with Rosaline, the resident ghost. It was going to be her performance piece. She was sleeping when I came upon her, and wasn't too happy when I woke her from her nap."

Alan didn't look too happy as Erica recounted her brush with the deceased, even if it was more happenstance than hard evidence.

"Did you catch her name?" he asked. "Maybe there was more than one Rosaline hunter."

"She didn't give it. She was young, pale, had black hair with bangs. And a bit of a temper."

"Her name was Jessa Craven," Alan said. "She found her way into advanced acting, so I met her at the beginning of the semester. Kind of a coup for a sophomore, but she deserved to be there. She's good. She was good," he said, correcting himself.

"And now what happens?" Erica asked.

"The grief counselors will be out in force tomorrow," he answered. "Classes are cancelled, and the theater is closed to anyone except the authorities until further notice."

"Cressida must be beside herself," said Erica.

"She must be. The text didn't come from her, but from her second in command, Luke Barton."

"Did I meet him at Cressida's party?" Erica asked.

"Probably," Alan replied. "They seem to travel together."

"Yes, now I remember," said Erica. "Someone standing near me described them as Morgan Le Fey and her Mordred. Not their biggest fan, I guess. Morgan was King Arthur's enemy."

"There's a range of opinion on that," Alan said. "That's only in the musical *Camelot*. In earlier versions of the myth, Morgan looks out for Arthur."

"But Mordred. Wasn't he Arthur's son?" Erica asked.

"Yes, and the musical skips that part," Alan said. "Mordred was the offspring of Arthur and his half-sister. Only Arthur didn't know that he was sleeping with his half-sister. Mordred felt that Arthur abandoned him as a father and vows to revenge himself on dear old Dad by bringing down Arthur and everything he had built. The Round Table included."

"Must have made for an awkward Father's Day," Erica interjected.

"Mordred had his Aunt Morgan put a spell on Arthur to keep him from coming home from the hunt one night," Alan continued. "During which time Lancelot and Guinevere got together."

"After years of soulful looks," Erica added.

"Something like that," he said. "Anyway, Mordred engineers it so that the unhappy couple are caught together. Lancelot is arrested and escapes. Guinevere is almost burned at the stake, and Lancelot rescues her as the flames are licking her toes. Everybody goes to war, Guinevere ends up in a convent, many knights die, but revive enough to stand and sing at the curtain call."

"Good for them," Erica said. "Everything I know, I learned from musicals."

"More than a few people around here would agree with you on that," said Alan. "And as far as Cressida and company are concerned, given that term limits have no meaning in the Theater Department, if Cressida is chair for life, then Luke can look forward to an equally long career here."

"And so can everyone who serves under them," said Erica, mostly to herself. "So Morgan and Mordred never slept together?" she asked, returning to the topic of discussion.

"Only in the Chicago company. Ba dum bum," answered Alan.

"Old joke," said Erica.

"New answer," Alan began. "No. Not in the myth or in the musical. Why do you ask?"

"I just wondered. The Morgan and Mordred comment I overheard, which started this little trip down musical memory lane. Cressida, I would put in the vast expanse of middle age, and Luke doesn't look to be there quite yet. Despite the age gap, not that it would make any difference, I wondered if those two . . ."

"Not that I've heard," said Alan. "And in Luke's case, there may be a difference more challenging than age."

"I see," Erica said. "Any confirmation on that?"

"Nothing definite," said Alan. "Just an educated guess. And believe me, I would have heard. They're a tight little group. No real difference between public and private information around this place."

"Well, maybe they are truly BFF's, besties for life. Or Cressida just wants a plus one for social occasions. I didn't see a Mr. McPheers at the party."

"There isn't one. At least, not in Canfield. She's divorced. And amply provided for, if that house is any indication."

"Nice house," Erica agreed. "Maybe she bought at a time when faculty could afford to buy around here. With or without spousal support. Or she's really good at playing the stock market."

"I'd prefer not to speculate on Cressida's speculation," Alan said. "Let's leave it at she lives in a nice house. Good for her. And Luke, well, good for him too, whatever their arrangement might be."

"And what are they saying about us and our *arrangement*?"

"We're still new in town, so not much."

"Let's keep it that way," Erica said. "So what do we do now?"

"There's a meeting tomorrow morning in a classroom near Cressida's office. The entire theater faculty is expected to be there, although I doubt they'll be much to report. Check your texts."

Erica found her phone under the menus. In addition to the text from the powers that be, there were a number of emails, mostly from students who wanted to know if it were true that classes were cancelled the next day. The millennials had been the first to hear the news, relying on an electronic network that moved faster than anything the baby boomers or even Gen Xers subscribed to. They had been among the first to know about their classmate's demise, which quickly followed the news about the fall production.

"One of my students tells me that the cast list is already up for *Hedda*," said Erica.

"The expected outcome, I suppose," said Alan.

"Not exactly," Erica replied. "Someone named Jessa got Hedda. Someone named Alexis gets to play her wimpy friend, Mrs. Elvsted."

"Jessa Craven?" asked Alan.

"The very one," Erica answered.

Chapter 6

The word 'happy' would lose its meaning if it were not balanced by sadness.
Carl Jung

The multitude had assembled and waited for their leader. In the face of the crisis, Cressida appeared to be calm, her usual put-together self, not a single well-coifed hair out of place. No students were in attendance, blessedly, so the call must not have gone out to them. Back in the day, when a student died at a place of higher learning, the institution dealt briefly with the media, and only if absolutely necessary. The sad event was quickly placed in a file under the catchall of an "internal investigation," otherwise known as "Don't Ask, Won't Tell." Even now, when social media ruled the earth, the administration could be reasonably confident that any interest in this sad news would last for a single news cycle, and then they could return to business as usual.

Eight minutes after the appointed hour, just as they do on the Broadway stage, an invisible curtain rose, and Cressida appeared front and center in the large classroom that had been chosen for this meeting. Normally, Cressida would have spoken from center stage, her usual nesting place, but the theater was off limits until further notice, and the shop padlocked, leaving the actors and the technical crew without a place to call home. The waiting would be agony.

From the back, which were the only seats available by the time she and Alan arrived, Erica expected

Cressida to launch into a stirring rendition of "Friends, Romans, Countrymen." Cressida opted instead for going straight to the point, which was not her usual direction.

"Hello, all," she began. "You know why I have called you here. A terrible thing happened on the stage of our beloved Brink. We need to talk about how to go forward after this tragedy. Although the autopsy on Ms. Craven has not been completed, I am told by the authorities that there are no outward signs of violence, thank goodness. We will await the official findings to know for sure, and I will certainly keep you posted.

After a brief pause, she continued. "I knew Jessa only a little, and she was a dear girl with a bright future ahead of her. So bright, in fact, that she had just been cast in the lead of our upcoming fall production. Quite a coup for a sophomore." Cressida nodded at Luke, standing off to her right, who was the director of the show and had done the casting. He nodded back. A muffled reaction wafted through the crowd, primarily from those who had not been alerted that the cast list was up.

"Now we must turn our attention to our students," Cressida continued. "They must be hurting even more than we are. They think themselves invulnerable at this age, then something like this happens. We can keep the real world at bay for only so long."

Erica had always found it odd when people insisted that students were in college to prepare them for living in the real world. Perhaps some did need this particular type of instruction. Even if they did not have to support themselves financially, which a number of them already did, most students lived in the real world and had done so for quite some time. The hard part was avoiding the real world, which could be found at the end of their arm in the form of their phone, to which they held tightly and which they surrendered only under duress.

"As we—Luke—said in the text, grief counselors are available to speak to any member of our community who would benefit from their services. Classes will resume, and rehearsals will go on as soon as we can make certain adjustments." Cressida's words were briefly interrupted by a whispered confab with Luke. She nodded to him before continuing.

"The work we do as artists, and what we try to pass on to our students, engenders a certain closeness within the theater community, whether here or on the professional stage. Our little band is no different. You should expect questions from students. Depending upon the information available and your own good judgment, you should feel free to answer them to the best of your ability. We have always encouraged the free exchange of ideas in our classes. We also need to keep in mind how best to serve the needs of our students and, at the same time, respect the privacy of the student's— Jessa's—family, which they have requested from the media and from the world at large."

Cressida paused, less for dramatic effect than simply to catch her breath. "I know I can trust your discretion, as I always have. And I would open the floor to questions if I had any more information to impart. But I don't, so I won't. I will keep everyone posted as the details emerge."

Cressida nodded to the group and left the room, with Luke right behind her. The crowd quickly dispersed. Although the circumstances that led to it were heartbreaking, a day off was a day off.

"So it's tell the students, but don't tell the students because there's nothing to tell the students?" Erica asked Alan as they took a leisurely walk through the campus, having no pressing engagements.

"Something like that," he said.

"Well, it's a plan," replied Erica.

"Erica, they're new at this," said Alan. "How would you explain a dead body found in the theater?"

"It's their question to answer," said Erica sharply. "I will leave it to them."

In the end, the students had no need to be at the meeting. They knew in less than seconds what had occurred, someone having texted out the minutes of the meeting as it was happening. A tight little community indeed, as the details of that fateful morning quickly emerged. The ghost light on the stage was off when a member of the technical staff, no doubt grumbling, entered the theater, found it in darkness, and crossed the stage to turn on the light. He also found Jessa slumped against the stage left wall, from which there was no exit. Apparently, she had found one.

Back in the day—the day being the 1800's—theaters were lit by gas. Wanting to avoid an explosion, the flame of a gas light stayed on even when there was no performance, in order to alleviate the pressure that could build up in the pipes and lead to combustion. Some believed that the gas-lit ghost light also kept the spirits away. Now the ghost light was lit by an electric bulb. Jessa's reason for being in the darkened theater was to experience a visit from Rosaline Vander Brink, patroness of the theater that bore her name. Erica wondered if they finally had a chance to meet, and now, would the two haunt the theater in tandem?

Chapter 7

The busy bee has no time for sorrow.
William Blake

It was always unclear what the mourning period
should be in circumstances like these. The college
decided that one day off from classes would be
sufficiently respectful, a show of genuine concern that
would not incite calls from parents about the
appropriate use of their tuition dollar. Given that the
day off was a Friday, little changed. Friday was the
least attended day of classes, with nothing scheduled
after 2 p.m., an arrangement that suited both students
and faculty. By Monday, when classes resumed, almost
everyone felt emotionally ready to move forward.

Two weeks after that, in Erica's Introduction to
Theater class, the topic of the day was the play *Hedda
Gabler*. It was still on the production schedule, so Erica
felt there was no reason to adjust the syllabus. After a
quick shifting of roles, Alexis found herself playing the
lead, where some felt she had always belonged,
although this was usually said in whispers. The student
playing the maid was moved to the role of Mrs. Elvsted.
A student who had auditioned on a lark, with no real
hope of being cast, was thrilled to discover that she
would be playing the maid, Berte, given her whoops of
joy when a revised cast list was posted.

Erica's class was discussing whether Hedda should
be viewed as a villain or a victim.

"If we're sticking to words starting with the letter V, why not add 'vixen' to the list?" asked Erica, after the students had chosen and defined the terms of the discussion. A lively conversation ensued as to whether this was too gender specific or demeaning to Hedda. After all, Eilert Lovberg, whom Hedda admires far more than her milquetoast husband George Tesman, frequents a brothel and drinks to excess, yet there was no equivalent term for his behavior, which society would condemn but tolerate. The discussion had lasted for most of the hour when a knock at the door abruptly silenced the conversation.

"Yes?" said Erica, expecting, at most, a brief interruption.

A slight figure entered the room and looked around. She had pale skin and dark hair with bluntly cut bangs, just like her sister. Also the same height, weight, and features. In fact, an exact duplicate. The class let out a collective gasp as a living reminder of the dead girl joined the class. It took all of her combined professional skill and will for Erica not to join them.

"Professor McPheers gave me this note for you," the student said, handing Erica a crumpled piece of paper.

On it Cressida has scribbled, "Let her sit in; I will explain later."

That helps, thought Erica, wondering at the same time if the student has perused the note.

"I'm a Bio major," the student said, explaining to Erica and to the group. "My sister was into theater, and I wanted to experience what she loved. I thought it would help me to understand . . . ." Her head lowered, the girl's words faded into nothingness. Erica picked up the thread with an easy question posed to her newest student.

"What is your name?" Erica asked, as gently as she could.

"Joy," the girl replied, lifting her head and looking straight at Erica.

"Welcome, Joy," Erica said. "You can take the seat over there, by the window."

When the class ended, Erica made a speedy trip to Cressida's office. She had offered to talk to Joy, who was off just as quickly, saying that she had a lab across campus but would check in later with Erica. Given that Joy was simply sitting in on the class, not even an official auditor, she was not required to do any of the work, so catching up on the reading would not be an issue. But there was nothing simple about it, which is why Erica made a beeline to speak with the woman who had bequeathed her an extra charge. Cressida was in and seeing people.

"Erica, I'm glad you stopped by," Cressida said, as if this were strictly a social call. "I guess you met Joy."

I did when she walked into my class unannounced, thought Erica, impressed by Cressida's ability to treat this as a matter of little consequence. For Cressida, maybe it was. Erica saw things differently, as did most of her students, who spent the final minutes sneaking a look at their new classmate as the class lumbered toward its finish.

"Yes, we met," Erica said with forced calm. "She seems nice. We didn't get much of a chance to talk, she had a Bio lab to go to. Why did she want to sit in on this class? Her sister wasn't even enrolled."

"She thinks it will help her to heal, and it was the only one that fit into her schedule. She won't enroll officially, she has no room in her schedule, and it's too late anyway. Whenever she can tear herself away from the Science Center, she would like to observe things over here, and live a little of the life that her sister did."

"What is she doing back at school so soon? Her sister died a couple of weeks ago—"

"I guess we all grieve in our own ways," Cressida said, cutting Erica off. "She seems like a pretty serious student—"

"Aren't all Bio majors serious students?" Erica shot back.

"As are Theater majors," Cressida insisted, her patience visibly waning. "To tell you the truth, she said that she could not stay in her parents' house one more minute. So maybe coming back here was the healthiest thing she could have done for herself."

"Cressida, you did notice that they are identical twins," Erica said.

"Yes, it's uncanny," Cressida admitted. "The absolute image of each other."

"So, we have someone who is an exact physical match to the deceased girl, and she's haunting the theater program for the rest of the semester?"

"Curious choice of words, but yes, Erica. Longer, if she wishes. We can hardly ban her from the Brink. The theater is open to everyone. And it's not her fault that she looks exactly like her sister."

Cressida was clearly tiring of this little chat. Then, as if by magic, Luke Barton appeared to remind Cressida of a meeting they both needed to attend. Somewhere else. *Now.* Erica wondered if Cressida had a button under her desk with which she summoned him, or if a chip had been implanted somewhere on his body, serving the same purpose. Either way, the two disappeared from the office. Cressida's parting message was simple and surprisingly direct: "Just be kind to her, Erica. I'm sure you can manage that."

"The poor girl walked smack dab into a discussion of *Hedda Gabler*," Erica told Alan when the two reconvened at the apartment later that day. "You know, the part her sister was supposed to play? And who knew she had a sister? The students clearly didn't. I thought I was about to face a mass coronary of 18 to 20 year old's. I might have thrown myself in too, just to vary the demographic."

"Why was she even there?" Alan asked.

"She told the class that she is a Bio major, but she wanted to experience what her sister loved. Cressida okayed her to sit in on a theater class—mine—even though we're way past the point of adding classes. And she doesn't seem to want to take the course. Just to be there."

"Was Jessa Craven enrolled in your class?" Alan inquired.

"No," said Erica. "That's the weird thing. There are multiple sections being taught. Cressida said that this was the only one that fit her schedule. I have a feeling that Cressida decided to dump this on the new kid, the part-timer."

"I doubt she would be that cavalier," said Alan. "Did you ask her?"

"Oh, yes," said Erica. "I went straight over, right after I finished teaching."

"And?" he asked, when Erica paused.

"Total nonchalance, followed by a hasty exit with Luke. To an undisclosed and possibly non-existent meeting. I'm guessing here, but knowing that this might require a gentle touch, Cressida may have opted for me because I have more experience than, say, Tasha. Or anyone else whose career they might actually care about. So I have been assigned short-term hand-holding duties."

"I'm sure Cressida hopes this will all blow over soon," Alan said. "For the department, anyway. For Jessa's sister, not so much. Then again," he added, "if she's a Bio major, don't they spend their lives in a lab?"

"Yes," Erica replied. "I checked, and she has a very full schedule, and is now sitting in on the Intro to

Theater course. So she can be where her sister was. Even if her sister was never actually there."

"It seems a small enough accommodation for the grieving sister," Alan said.

"Sure, okay, I agree," said Erica. "And Joy—her name is Joy, by the way—will probably have had enough before too long and go back to the land of beakers and test tubes. Where the answers are clear cut. No levels of interpretation, like in Theater, or in English classes, for that matter."

"Here's hoping," Alan offered. "But you do know that even science isn't really a science. There's more art in there than people give it credit for."

"Fine, so everyone's an artist," Erica replied. "I just hope our little scientist finds what she's looking for. Whatever that is."

"With you as her escort," Alan began, "how could she fail?"

Later that night, a text circulated among the theater faculty. The autopsy had been completed. Anaphylactic shock had been determined to be the official cause of death, due to an extreme allergic reaction. To what, it didn't say. The students received the news as quickly as their professors, a few much sooner than those faculty members who might read their email—it was almost a job requirement—but refused to read or send a text. Maybe the students sent out the text in the first place. If not in charge of the asylum, the inmates seemed to have a strong voice in running it.

Chapter 8

Such bees! Bilbo had never seen anything like them. "If one were
to sting me," he thought, "I should swell up as big as I am!"
J.R.R. Tolkien

Given that the focus of the last class had quickly
shifted from Hedda, who burned the manuscript of the
man she loved, destroying him in the process, to Joy,
whose sister was supposed to play Hedda, Erica
decided to have the students write about the title
character to prove to herself that something had sunk in.
She asked the students to offer an interpretation of
Hedda as villain, victim, vixen, or call her what you
will. Since students tended to make everything about
themselves, Erica reminded the class that Hedda was
not some mean girl they knew in high school. Hedda
may be a mean girl, but even she had to answer to
Judge Brack, who gains power over her through
blackmail. Oh, and Hedda lived in the nineteenth
century, when the rules were different. Reputation was
everything in Hedda's world. One false step and there
was no getting your good name back. So Hedda may be
brave and bold within the confines of her own home,
which she rarely left, yet not so willing to do anything
that might sully the reputation of the woman who had
more freedom as General Gabler's daughter than
Professor Tesman's wife.

Erica had the students write their answers in class in
order to get their interpretation and not an analysis
courtesy of the internet. To this end, she made them
actually write it. "I can read anything," she had insisted

to students who offered the excuse of poor handwriting in order to compose on their laptops. This might have left Joy with nothing to do, given that she had not read the play, but the student busily wrote something, just like everyone else.

When Erica got to Joy's answer, it was not like anyone else's. Joy asked and answered a question of her own, one that would undoubtedly be on her mind. It read:

"My sister and I were identical twins. That means we looked alike, but it means more than the surface stuff. I'm not talking about some psychic connection that enabled us to read each other's thoughts. Everyone with the same parents shares the same gene pool. My sister and I shared the same embryo. With identical twins, everyone believes that we were exactly the same in the DNA department. We may have started out that way, but science now tells us that although our genes are very similar, they are not necessarily identical.

"I don't want to go all Bio major on you, but there are things called epigenetic factors, like environment or diet or exposure to cigarette smoke, which can cause differences between identical twins. We grew up in the same house. We ate the same food. Nobody smoked. As sisters, we were close, but very different. She was an actress and I'm a scientist.

Nobody pushed me toward science or Jessa toward the stage. We found our own way there. But genetic factors can result in one twin getting a disease while the other one remains healthy. One has an allergy, which the other one doesn't."

After this mostly scientific discussion, Joy saved the most gripping part for the finish, asking, "Do you know what it's like to die of anaphylactic shock?"

"I looked it up," she wrote. "Sometimes, when there's an allergic reaction, it can begin with hives, and a little Benadryl will take care of it. The rash fades. Things rapidly get worse if your face starts to swell. Then you need to get to an EpiPen in a hurry. The injection of adrenaline should stop the allergic reaction. If that doesn't work, you better be on your way to the nearest emergency room, hopefully in an ambulance, where they can keep your airway open if your throat closes up and you stop breathing. At the hospital, you will receive another dose of adrenaline, this time through an IV, followed by steroids. With any luck, this works. If not, then you're in heavy duty trouble. Your heart could stop. If the blood isn't pumping, your body shuts down. It's almost over.

"And what is it like to die alone, in an empty theater, on a pile of rope, having a reaction to an allergy you never knew you had? Confusing and scary. Beyond confusing and scary. Terrifying. And you know what else my twin and I had in common? Neither of us had any allergies. None that we knew of. None that I knew of. Not a sneeze between us. Ever. So she never knew what was happening to her until it was too late. And there was nobody there to help her. Least of all, me."

Erica put Joy's paper back in the pile. She was unsure how to react. Should she sound an alarm? Contact someone in the Counseling Center? Let Cressida know? From her brief conversation with the chair of the Theater Department, Erica was fairly certain that the less Cressida knew, the better Cressida liked it. And there was always Luke Barton to extricate her from anywhere she preferred not to be. Cressida had already been an unhelpful first stop. And although Joy found herself in impossible circumstances, she seemed to be dealing with them in a calm, rational manner, at least as far as Erica could tell. Maybe this was just the way Bio majors talked, even in moments of distress. Erica decided to take a wait-and-see approach with Joy, and insist upon a conversation after their next class meeting.

Chapter 9

Beedle dee, dee dee dee
Two ladies
Beedle dee, dee dee dee
And I'm the only man
Ja!
Fred Ebb

"I wonder if all of her essays look like that," Alan
said after reading Joy's response. "Obviously, it would
be on her mind."

"Well, it's a harder sell if this is what you turn in as
a lab report," said Erica.

"Unless her field is immunology," said Alan.

"It probably will be, if it's not already," Erica
replied.

The two had met for coffee before Alan headed off
to rehearse some of the seniors on their audition pieces.
The Blanches would have to present more than one
monologue to most graduate schools, something
classical as well as contemporary, and might also be
expected to sing at least sixteen bars of a song of their
choosing. In less than three minutes for each item, they
would need to prove their worth to programs that would
accept maybe two out of one-hundred applicants. Lotsa
luck, ladies.

Although new to the theater faculty and only a one-
semester visitor, Erica was free to wander where she
chose. Later that afternoon, she found herself among
the rehearsal rooms that dotted the hallway leading to
the theater. These rooms were in high demand for those
working on scenes or songs. Students were not allowed

to congregate unless their names were next on the tightly scheduled list. None of the rooms was entirely soundproof, so musical rehearsals, in particular, were heard by all, including those waiting in the hallway. As Erica passed by, she heard someone singing, a lilting soprano, and she knew that she was hearing the genuine article. There are talented singers who can hit all the notes and infuse meaning into their musical expression. As you listen, you can see and hear all the work and the training that went into achieving this end. And it is good, it is still good, even if the effort shows. Then there are the songbirds who just open their mouths and sing. Not that songbirds—the human ones—do not need work and training to produce the sound that they do, but it has a natural resonance, not a studied effort. Even listening from the hallway, Erica knew that this singer was a songbird.

Erica checked the name on the schedule, and it began with Ashley. For simplicity sake, Alan had come up with an easy way to distinguish between the trio. Alexis is the one who acts, Ashley is the one who sings, Ava is the one who is funny. So this was Ashley. *My Fair Lady* had been announced as the spring musical, and Erica was almost sorry she would miss it. Erica knew that *Camelot* had been considered and rejected, given the few female roles and dearth of ladies in waiting on the cast list. *My Fair Lady* could make use of as many flower sellers, fine ladies, prostitutes, and dance hall girls needed to accommodate the flood of auditioners who would arrive with varying degrees of ability. Ashley would undoubtedly be Eliza Doolittle. She would do her proud.

Erica moved on down the hallway to investigate other corners of the theater. She lingered for a moment when she heard a group of students talking and laughing as they approached Ashley's rehearsal room.

Erica was close enough to hear their conversation but far enough away not to be part of it.

"You're going to be a great Eilert," said one the two females to the student whom Erica recognized as Mercury, the one who'd arrived seemingly unbidden to help Erica and Alan move into their apartment. Alan later told Erica that the student's name was Kellan Pierson, an actor, of course, though his name had no meaning for her until now.

"I know," Kellan replied, then added, "with you as Hedda." The two smiled at each other in a way that suggested more than a professional partnership.

Okay, now we're getting somewhere, thought Erica, since Alan's thumbnail descriptions of his students rarely did them justice. With Alexis and Kellan identified, and the songbird Ashley still trilling away in the rehearsal room, the final member of the trio had to be Ava, the comedian. Ava didn't seem to be in the mood to laugh nor to be the cause of laughter in others.

"It's not funny," she began. "Think about how you got that part, Alexis."

"Talent?" Alexis replied with a dramatic toss of her hair.

"Because someone died," Ava insisted.

Alexis and Kellan's grins quickly turned to glares as they stared down the third member of their party.

"They would have figured out their mistake soon enough," said Kellan. "A sophomore? Please. She could never compete with our Alexis. I don't know why they cast her in the first place."

"Talent?" Ava repeated, minus the hair toss.

"I don't know what they were thinking," said Alexis. "Why do you care?"

"I don't care," said Ava, quickly capitulating. "You and Kell will be great, but someone died in order for this to happen. I don't think we should forget that."

"I don't see the faculty wearing black armbands," said Alexis, as Kellan nodded his agreement. "They want to be done with it. We should follow their lead. For once," she said, smirking at Kellan, who added, "like that's gonna happen." This led to another meaningful smile between the two of them, with Ava the odd woman out, though it was Kellan who broke the mood.

"Hey, Baby Cakes, your time's up," Kellan shouted through the door of the rehearsal room. The singing abruptly stopped. Erica would have much preferred the musical solo to the scene playing out in the hallway. Ashley, appearing at the door, was revealed to be an intriguing combination of Asian and American, though more American than Asian if her short, bleached blonde hair was a clue to her identity.

"Avy here can't hold it anymore," Kellan added, "We gotta go."

Ava, her freckles almost camouflaging the embarrassed blushes that suffused her face, exchanged a look with Ashley, who quickly closed the door to the rehearsal room and joined them.

As they walked away, Erica wondered how this herd truly operated, plus or minus the erstwhile Mercury. Each had her own area in which to shine, so maybe it was their separate talents that kept this alliance from turning into an episode of *Survivor*. The dueling Blanches might tell that tale. But sooner than later, the herd would graduate, and it would be every doe for herself. Was each deer incomplete without the herd?

Chapter 10

The pedigree of Honey
Does not concern the bee;
A clover, any time, to him
Is aristocracy.
Emily Dickinson

Several days later, Erica found herself in the copy room, generating a few last minute pages for her class. Erica still went old school when it came to copies and distributed something students could hold in their hands. Although this information would make its way to the class website after it had been discussed in class, she did not post things exclusively online. That day would undoubtedly come. For now, she didn't want to give her students another reason to stare at a screen.

Erica entered the copy room to see Tasha Cooper, the new drama professor whom Erica had met at Cressida's getting-to-know-you party but had seen little of since. The first semester at a new teaching job most closely resembles being shot out of a cannon, although, from the look of her, Tasha seemed to be taking it all in her stride. She was chatting with another young woman when Erica walked in, someone who also had the look of a new assistant professor, both in age and level of eagerness. Tasha introduced her as Daphne Nowiki, who had arrived at Canfield as a visiting assistant professor in BioChemistry. Many colleges now opted for visiting professorships. They could try out a recent Ph.D., often among the best and the brightest, for a three-year term, after which the position might be converted to tenure track, possibly after another search. The department could also find itself another newly minted Ph.D. for another three-year slot. Always more where they came from.

Tasha invited Erica to join her and Daphne for coffee. Since she had just enough time before class, Erica joined them, after making 50 copies of her document. This is how friendships are formed in academe, over the copy machine followed by a quick cup of coffee.

Making their way to the nearest coffee shop of the several on campus, they found a table that would accommodate the three of them, their books, bags, and tall lattes. There were few students in attendance. At this hour of the morning, most were either asleep or in class, hopefully not both.

Erica learned that Daphne was not Polish as the name Nowicki might suggest. Professionally, she was known by her maiden name, Stephenson. On the Canfield campus, you had little choice in how you were listed. Your married name was your name, although you could hyphenate your married and maiden names if you thought to ask and your request was made firmly enough. Stephenson-Nowicki was more of a mouthful than Daphne wanted just to make a point, so, for the time being, she was Nowicki. Daphne explained that her husband worked in the administration as a development officer, so her connection to the school might extend longer that the initial three years of her contract if the school were still paying at least one of them.

"We were discussing Topic A when you came by," said Tasha once they were seated.

"Which Topic A would that be?" asked Erica.

"The death in the theater," Tasha said. "Is there another one?"

"Oh, that one, of course," Erica replied. "It's just that Topic A's seems to come and go so fast around here, displaced by the latest news on who did or did not get cast in the spring production."

"I've noticed that," said Tasha. "Short attention span theater."

"I was thinking the same thing," said Daphne. "Of course, a chemist can't say that."

"Why not?" asked Erica and Tasha in unison.

"You can trash your own department but not someone else's?" Daphne answered.

"Probably true," said Tasha, as Erica nodded. "But closer to your turf than ours. Tell Erica what you heard about the cause of death."

"Well, we all heard it was anaphylactic shock," Daphne began. "That was known pretty quickly. What the poor girl was allergic to took more time to determine. From what they're saying in the Science Center, it was a bee sting."

"How would a bee get into the theater, especially at this time of year?" Erica wanted to know. "Don't bees usually do their thing in the spring and summer when the flowers are blooming?"

"Don't look at me," said Tasha. "My knowledge of bees begins and ends with *The Secret Lives of Bees*. With the image of the Virgin Mary as a black woman, the Black Madonna, on the side of a jar of honey. I wasn't paying a lot of attention to the actual bees."

"You're way ahead of me," said Erica, who turned to Daphne, asking, "I know you said you were a chemist, but do you know anything about bees?"

"Quite a lot, actually," Daphne admitted. "Bees collect pollen from their favorite plants. The flowers bloom when their pollinators, the bees, arrive, so they kind of work in unison. Bees aren't limited to one season. In the spring and summer, they feed off different flowers. They are still around in the fall, when the temperatures get colder. Then, they begin to prepare for hibernation and the long winter ahead."

"They settle their brain for a long winter's nap?" asked Erica.

"'Twas the night before Christmas," said Tasha. "Otherwise known as 'A Visit from St. Nicholas.' Next time, try a hard one."

Daphne looked perplexed, so Erica explained. "Occupational hazard. Those of us who teach literature tend to quote a lot. Mostly to amuse ourselves. Sorry. You were saying?"

"Okay," said Daphne, sounding unconvinced. "Bees hibernate in the winter, but not in the usual way. Like bears, for example. Bees stay active within the hive, generating their own heat by creating a cluster that protects the queen at the center of the cluster. The cluster eats the honey and shivers to generate heat."

"I know I'd be shivering," said Tasha. "With only the bees to keep me warm."

"It works for them," Daphne insisted. "So a stray bee can occasionally be sighted on a warm winter's day. Although around here, we don't get too many of those."

"Right," said Tasha. "And we were well into fall when, you know—"

"I think the administration is referring to it as 'the unfortunate accident,'" Erica offered.

"She didn't fall off a ladder, thank goodness," Tasha replied. "I'm not sure which category accidental death by bee falls into."

"Try fundraising around the news that a student died. It's a disaster, or so my husband tells me," Daphne said. "And you know that they keep bees on campus."

"They *what*?" said Erica and Tasha together. "Where do they keep them?" Erica managed to sputter out.

"At the apiary, of course," Daphne answered, as if this were common knowledge. "It's on the other side of campus. I help to supervise the students who work there. I'd be happy to give you a tour at some point."

"And we have an apiary because...?" Tasha wanted to know.

"Because the bee population has been dying out for a while now," Daphne said. "For any number of environmental factors. I won't bore you with the details, but suffice it to say that we are doing our bit to help the bees survive so that they can do what they do. So the world still has flowers and all sorts of food that we wouldn't have without the little pollinators."

Looking as though they were still digesting this information, Erica and Tasha had nothing to offer, so Daphne continued. "Plus, we sell the honey. It doesn't make a lot of money, but it supports the apiary and helps with some scholarships."

"That's always good," said Erica, recovering first. "The weird thing is that Joy, the twin sister of the dead girl, told me that neither of them had ever experienced an allergic reaction to anything in their lives. And an allergy to bee stings is something you tend to know about early on. Pretty much the first time you've been stung. How could she not know?"

"That's the weird thing?" asked Tasha. "How about a bee got into a closed theater and managed to sting a girl who didn't know she was allergic?"

"How about that she had an identical twin who's sitting in on one of my classes?" Erica said. No one had an immediate response. After a quick look at her watch, Erica had an answer.

"I've got to go teach," she said. "Daphne, a pleasure to meet you. Tasha, don't be a stranger. See you both soon, I hope," she added, while grabbing her things and beating a hasty exit. Any more discussion of the not-so-secret lives of bees would have to wait for another day.

Chapter 11

To be successful, one has to be one of three bees—the queen
bee, the hardest working bee, or the bee that does not fit in.
Suzy Kassem

At the end of the next class hour, Erica asked Joy to
stay with an offhand "a moment of your time?" This put
Joy first in line to speak with her. Erica simply wanted
to nail down an hour when the two could meet. There
were always students wanting to speak with her after
class, more from an emotional need than an intellectual
one, often without a real question to be asked. Because
Joy had been discreetly summoned, Erica's most
frequent visitor, a freshman named Trent, would have
to go second. Trent appeared to be having some
difficulty making the transition from high school to
college, but he was doing better in Erica's class than he
thought. Still, touching base seemed essential to his
well being. For today, whatever was on his mind would
have to wait.

When Erica suggested to Joy that the two have a
conversation after this class, the student politely
declined with the excuse that she had to go work in the
apiary.

"They have monkeys here?" asked Trent,
overhearing, and sounding enthusiastic about the
prospect. Joy turned to him and explained that an apiary
was where they kept bees, not any member of the ape
family, which she referred to as hominoids. She also
gave Trent a look that suggested that he might be a not-

so-distant cousin. From endless crossword puzzles, Erica knew that aviaries were dedicated to birds, but her knowledge on this subject was limited. Were it not for her previous conversation with Daphne, Erica might have asked the same question. She was grateful that Trent had jumped in first.

"We keep bees because the bee population is dying out," Joy continued. "If the bees are dying out, then so are the flowers that rely on bees for pollination. Not to mention up to a third of all the food on the planet, which we owe to the pollinating bees. There's been a decline in the number of bees since the 1990's with lots of reasons why this is happening. It could be due to pesticides that kill bees, or to the parasites that feed on bees, or it could be climate change. Probably all three."

Erica noticed that Joy's answer was similar to Daphne's but more detailed. Erica wondered if everyone who worked at the apiary had to memorize the same answer to explain its existence. The discussion of anything that happened before he was born would usually be considered ancient history, but Trent listened in rapt attention.

"Can anyone help with the bees on campus?" he asked.

"They're always looking for people," Joy answered. "It requires some training. You wear protective gear that covers you from head to toe, hands and fingers included. And you need to be careful. Bees can still sting."

The mention of bee stings might have caused Joy pain, but she showed none. Trent, on the other hand, could have been imagining himself in a veiled safari hat and the type of coat and gloves more suitable for one of the first owners of a Model T. Whether it was the prospect of sporting this ensemble or finding a place for himself on campus, Trent was fully on board.

"Can I come over with you now?" Trent asked. Shaking him would not be easy, and Joy did not even try.

"Sure," she said with less enthusiasm than he showed.

"Cool beans," he said, and followed her out of the room with an eagerness that would make most puppies look blasé by comparison.

Given that the students in line were getting restless, it was just as well that Joy and Trent had relinquished their places. Still, Joy left without confirming an appointment. Then again, that's what email is for. Erica would follow up later.

Chapter 12

The moan of doves in immemorial elms,
And murmuring of innumerable bees.
Alfred, Lord Tennyson

Erica quickly followed up with Daphne to arrange a trip to the apiary.

"One of my students mentioned working at the apiary, and I wondered what was involved. I hope this is not imposing, but do you think you could give me a tour? Are non-beekeepers allowed to visit?" Erica had asked in her email to Daphne, who replied that she would be happy to show Erica around. A date and time were arranged.

As they walked toward the apiary, Erica was impressed by the rows of man- or woman-made hives that she saw in the distance. Extra-curricular activities were expanding—whatever made the students happy and kept them from transferring—but she did not expect to find beekeeping on the same list as Pilates and Mixed Martial Arts.

"Bee hives are naturally occurring," Daphne began. "You see them hanging from high places, like the corner of a roof on a house. You can also find them in the hollow of a tree. As you know, the bee population has had a precipitous drop over the past few years. We're doing what we can to help them survive. Let's stay in the warehouse and watch from here," she said, pointing to the long narrow building before them. When they entered, Erica could see a row of windows that ran the length of a room. There were wire shelves on one of the side walls of the warehouse, holding honey in unlabeled jars. By the door, a series of hooks held the beekeepers' uniforms—coats, veiled hats, and gloves— in a variety of sizes.

"I'm just as glad to watch from here," said Erica, who had no plans to get up close and personal with the buzzing population. "Are you one of the beekeepers?" she asked Daphne. "I wouldn't have thought that a chemist—"

"Bio-Chem, actually," Daphne replied. "I'm new, so I pitch in where I can. It's actually pretty interesting. And you get to know students in a different way, see them in a different light. The students in my classes I know, but students outside the sciences also sign up for this. I'm getting to know them too."

Erica wondered how Daphne could tell them apart once the beekeeper had donned the appropriate attire. Only by height, if that. She also wondered if Daphne had made the acquaintance of young Trent, or Joy, for that matter. For the time being, Erica was more interested in the hives than in their keepers.

"Erica, you are about to learn more about bees than you ever wanted to know. It will be just the essentials, I promise, but tell me when you've had enough," said Daphne.

"Will do," Erica replied. "And I really appreciate your doing this. Professional courtesy goes only so far."

"Glad to do it," Daphne said and seemed to mean it, as they walked toward the windows to observe the beekeepers on their rounds.

"Okay, so those boxes on top of one and other are the hives," Daphne said.

"I'm with you so far," Erica answered. "I don't suppose they can be purchased at your nearest Container Store?"

"Oh, no," Daphne said with a laugh. "It would require something more specialized. Are you planning to set something up?"

"No," said Erica firmly. "Just looking, at this point."

"Right. Well, inside the hives are the honey combs, the hexagonal cells made up of beeswax on frames that slide in and out of the hive. They store food—honey and pollen being popular menu items—or house the next generation of bees in their various gestational forms: egg, larva, or pupa."

These words rang a bell that was quickly silenced. Erica flashed back to high school Biology and all the information she had forgotten since then. Daphne soldiered on.

"In the slow season—the winter months—a hive holds about 5,000 bees. It's ten times that number in the summer."

Erica simply nodded as she absorbed this information.

"Now, this part you'll like, Erica. At the top of the bee hierarchy is the queen, followed by the worker bees and the drones."

"Sounds a lot like the Theater Department," said Erica.

"Faculty or students?" Daphne asked quizzically.

"Both," said Erica. "Separate hierarchies on the same model. Who answers to whom, I haven't figured out yet."

"Sounds interesting," said Daphne.

"We'll see," said Erica. "Sorry for the interruption. Back to the bees."

"Okay. The queen lays the eggs, busy girl. She and only she gives birth to the worker bees, which are female and sometimes lay eggs, and the drones, which aren't and can't. For an egg to become a queen, it has to be exposed to royal jelly, which is creamy and white and produced in the glands of worker bees. The future queen, known as the virgin queen, gets her own special place, the 'queen cell,' and consumes more of the royal jelly as she develops."

"Yum," said Erica. "Sounds delicious."

"Well, the bees like it," Daphne replied. "All the larvae feast on royal jelly, but after three days, that's it for the drones and the worker bees, who develop more slowly than the queen. The queen will become a bee-making machine that lays eggs days and night, about 2000 in April and May, then nothing over the winter if there's no nectar or anything else to feed on. If they're really low on food, the drones are shown the door. The drones are the daddies, and during her mating flight, the queen breeds with drones from a number of hives, including her own. Unfortunately for the drones, an essential body part, the endophallus, is ripped out as they mate in mid-air, and the drone dies."

"No real upside to being a drone, is there?" asked Erica.

"I don't think they have a choice," Daphne answered. "Now, the queen may be the largest bee in the hive, but she has a smaller brain and can't even feed herself. Luckily, she is surrounded by worker bees to keep her from starving."

"That's nice of them," said Erica. "So it's good to be the queen?"

"Yes and no," said Daphne. "Yes, they wait on her, hand and foot. Yes, because she is always surrounded by her court—"

"Her ladies in waiting?" Erica asked.

"More like bodyguards," Daphne answered. "And no, because all she does is lay eggs, all day every day, for the length of her reign. That 'nuptial flight' is one of the few times she leaves the hive during her lifespan, with 3-4 years being a pretty good run for a queen.

That's unless she can't fulfill her task and becomes a non-producing member of the bee colony," Daphne admitted. "Then the worker bees will most likely kill her—"

"Harsh," Erica interjected.

"Without a producing queen, the colony dies out," Daphne finished.

"Harsh but necessary, I guess," Erica said.

"The queen may lay a lot of eggs, but she has no maternal instinct. None at all," Daphne continued.

"So . . . nannies?" Erica wanted to know.

"Sort of," Daphne replied. "Among the queen's attendants are what are known as 'nurse bees,' which are worker bees, of course. They see to the new arrivals as they develop."

"Thank goodness for the help," Erica said.

"Yes. The most important thing to remember is that a hive can have only one queen. At a time," said Daphne.

"Got it," Erica replied.

"As I said, the queen bee stays in the hive for almost all of her lifespan," Daphne said. "Although there is an exception to that rule. If the queen feels that things are too crowded in the hive, she will leave, and the other bees will follow her to find a new hive to populate. This is what is called a swarm. Think of the swarm as moving day."

"I thought being swarmed meant being attacked by bees. Killer bees, usually," Erica began.

"I think I saw that movie," Daphne said. "In reality, bees are social animals amongst themselves. While they communicate with each other, they really aren't looking for human companionship. The connection to the hive is essential. If they become separated from the colony, they die. So they will attack if they feel that the hive is being threatened. Other than that, it's pretty much live and let live."

Erica nodded, taking it all in.

"Now, onto the hives," Daphne continued. "Our hives, in particular."

"I'm ready," Erica said.

"Okay, here we go. Each of the white boxes you see out there, stacked on top of each other, holds about seven to ten frames. When they are full, another story is added. Usually, there is a screened board at the bottom of the hive. It's easy access for the bees and helps to keep out the mites that could invade and destroy the colony."

"So mite control is a thing with bees?" Erica asked.

"Gotta keep them out," said Daphne. "To keep the hive healthy."

"And a healthy hive is—"

"Alive," said Daphne, with emphasis.

"Understood," Erica asserted.

"And there is a new threat on the horizon," Daphne added. "Murder hornets."

"What now?" said Erica. "Is that a joke? Or even a real thing?"

"Very real to the bees," said Daphne in all seriousness. "Their thing is to grab a honeybee, bite its head off, and bring the body home to feed its young. They originated in Asia, haven't been sighted here yet, but a few have been seen in the Pacific Northwest. One was definitely a queen, which could mean the start of a hive."

"And how do these hornets feel about people?" Erica asked.

"They tend to stay away from them. When they do sting, it can be fatal. About 50 deaths a year."

"But Jessa wasn't—"

"No," said Daphne, cutting off Erica's question. "They haven't made it to this neck of the woods. Probably only a matter of time...."

Visions of murder hornets danced in Erica's head until she broke the silence with "On that cheery note, tell me more about our own happy hives."

"Well, depending on the season, there are different tasks for beekeepers," Daphne began. "In the winter, you never open the hive. There are pictures of snow-covered hives decorated for the holidays. When the weather begins to warm up in spring, it's time to check the hive. Do the bees need anything, like more food, or are they still consuming what they stored from the previous winter? Summer is the busy season, for the bees anyway. It's important to remember that every time you open the hive and pull out a frame, productivity stops because the bees are paying more attention to the beekeeper than their own tasks. A smoker can be used to calm the bees when the hive is opened because smoke calms the bees."

"Who knew?" asked Erica.

"Beekeepers," Daphne answered. "The fall is the best time to collect the honey, which works perfectly for us, since that's when the students arrive and can get involved in the collecting and bottling of the honey."

"Is there an expiration date for honey?" Erica wondered for the first time in her life.

"Actually, there is," Daphne answered. "About two years from the time it's bottled."

"All those bottles on the wall have no labels," said Erica, turning and pointing in their direction. "How do you keep track?"

"There's a system," Daphne said. "We know which shelves were harvested when. Those bottles are fresh. They haven't been labeled yet, but they soon will be," she continued. "The students do it. We usually assign this to our baby beekeepers. That's what the newest recruits are called. And everything is done under supervision. Someone oversees all the activity in the apiary."

"Except for the bee that got away," said Erica.

"All the student activity, then," Daphne said. "This building is locked at night, so the honey is safe. I can't imagine anyone going near the hives without protective gear. All of that is locked up too."

Erica sincerely hoped this were true.

"Now for the harvesting," Daphne said. Erica also hoped this explanation would be the compressed version. Luckily, it was. Daphne explained that when the frames were lifted, one by one from the hive, the honey was separated from the beeswax and placed into a spinning extractor, then into a strainer that eliminated the remaining bits of dead bees or pieces of flowers. From there the honey went into bottles, like those currently placed on the shelves nearby. After this final detail, the explanation ended, and so did the tour.

Erica offered her genuine thanks to Daphne for taking the time to go through the life of the hive. Vague plans to get together, perhaps with their significant others, were mentioned. Leaving Daphne behind to attend to some bee-related matters, Erica made her way back to the main part of campus. On her way out of the building, she passed a tall beekeeper in the process of shedding the gear that protected the individual from harm but also shielded his or her identity. The removal of the veiled hat revealed a face that Erica recognized. It was Kellan, who was clearly a fan of queen bees in all their incarnations. Having caught his act outside the rehearsal rooms, Erica was beginning to see that this Mercury was everywhere, gathering intel, his own form of nectar, to report back to the three queens he served. Exactly why they would care about bees was beyond her, although she had a clearer idea of the form of recompense he received for his efforts.

Kellan nodded at Erica as she walked by. She passed him without comment.

Chapter 13

Sisters, sisters,
There were never such devoted sisters.
Irving Berlin

Having spent enough time in beeland to last her a while, Erica returned to the territory that was more comfortable or at least more familiar—the land of plays. Having finished with Hedda Gabler, whom many of the students decided was, in fact, just like that mean girl they knew in high school, Erica moved on to Chekhov and *Three Sisters*. Chekhov can be indecipherable the first time out, which she readily admitted to the students.

"I remember my first encounter with Chekhov. My first reaction was 'What the heck?' though I don't think that *heck* was the word I used. All those Russian names! Why does everyone have to have three names, plus a nickname? And there was no particular plot. I'm all for a play being character-driven, but what is it with these people? Nothing happens, and no one seems to change. I knew Chekhov was supposed to be a big deal in drama, but I just didn't get it. Not at first. Then, after reading more of his plays, I began to understand what he was getting at. We use the term 'naturalism,' which Eugene O'Neill would call 'the real realism.' More on O'Neill later. For Chekhov, it's all about showing characters in a way that is not necessarily theatrical but relies more on subtext, that which is not spoken. Someone could be asking someone else to 'Please pass the butter,' while their entire world is collapsing.

"I don't think anyone asks for the butter in this play. The sisters' dearest wish is get out of the provincial town in which they have been living, where they have been stuck, and go back to Moscow. To Moscow! To Moscow! You may ask, why don't they just go there? It's more complicated than getting the train fare."

Erica knew that Chekhov's world would be foreign to her students. With sisters, on the other hand, they should be on solid ground, even if they didn't have any. It was a way into the play, or so Erica hoped.

Joy already knew the way. When the students were asked to write about the relationship between the sisters Prozorova, Joy had an answer that scarcely mentioned the play. Instead, she wrote what she knew:

"Let me tell you about sisters. My sister and I were as close as close can be. But we were also as different.

"People think that because she was an actress and she could perform in front of hundreds of people, she was the brave one. I was the nerd who locked herself away in the science lab.

"Appearances can be deceiving, even if they are identical.

"My sister was a terrific actress, which I knew from the second grade when she played Sleeping Beauty and I was a thorn bush. Not jealous, really. I love science and always have. But getting her out on that stage was something else. It was more than stage fright. It was life fright.

"We used to dress alike. It wasn't enough that we looked alike, we had to dress the same every day. Definitely not my idea. Our mother had dressed us alike forever. Even she gave up by the time we got to high school. Not Jessa. She still needed it. Down to the last detail. If she wanted to curl her hair that day, I had to curl mine too. When it came to college, I drew the line. No more dressing alike. Even in high school, other

students laughed—and not in a good way—when we
showed up. I was not going through college in identical
outfits. I told Jessa that I would go to another school if
she kept this up. Jessa wanted to come here for the
Theater Department, but I had other options. She finally
said okay to not dressing alike, and then totally freaked
when the housing office wouldn't let us be roommates
freshman year. I pity the poor girl assigned to Jessa. I
heard she transferred. As sophomores, we can choose
our own roommates. There was nothing they could do
to stop us, I mean, stop Jessa, so—together again. It
was no easy gig. I was on call 24/7.

"It didn't matter whether she was getting through a
class or going to an audition. If she thought she had
taken on more than she could handle, she was on the
phone or texting. Jessa would call me when she was
down, and I would buck her up. It's always been that
way. It was like she was my perpetual shadow. Now,
she always will be.

"Sisters, sisters, sisters. They will never get to
Moscow. So what? Maybe that's what Chekhov thought
too. Just get on with it, girls."

Joy had stopped there. Erica hoped that getting it out
on paper, some of it, anyway, was doing her some
good. Erica didn't know if it was progress or just plain
sad that she referred to her sister in the past tense.
Clearly, Jessa's memory was very much alive. Erica
was intrigued by one line in particular: "She would call
me when she was down and I would buck her up." Jessa
had chosen to sleep alone in a deserted theater, waiting
for a ghost to appear. A misguided adventure, and one
that would frighten the heartiest of souls, which Jessa,
apparently, was not. At some point in the evening, Jessa
must have called on her sister for moral support, which
led Erica to only one conclusion.

Joy was in the theater the night her sister died.

Chapter 14

> *When, like the bee, tolling from every flower*
> *The virtuous sweets,*
> *Our thighs with wax, our mouths with honey pack'd,*
> *We bring it to the hive, and, like the bees,*
> *Are murd'red for our pains.*
> William Shakespeare

Few details seeped out of the ongoing investigation by the college, which proceeded in tandem with the local police department, another institution that was beyond circumspect in its discretion. Both had a vested interest in keeping the inquiry low key. A death, even accidental, on either of their watches, could be disastrous for their respective reputations. Parents expected those in authority to keep their offspring safe.

Upon closer inspection, it has been discovered that on the night in question, the stage was lightly dusted with a substance identified as bee pollen. There were no footprints to be found because the trail of pollen was smeared, obscuring any possible clues to its source. It was also known that Jessa was sitting upright when she was found, against the stage left wall, the one with no exit. If she had been able to sit up, it was odd that she had not thought to remove the stinger from her leg. Erica shared all of these details with Alan as soon as she heard them, from her students, of course. The students seemed to be better versed on the case than most of the faculty and nearly all of the residents of Canfield, especially if they were looking to the local paper for information. After reporting that a death had occurred on campus due to an allergic reaction, any discussion of the details of the case had been dropped. The paper knew what would be of interest to its readers, and this wasn't it. The relationship between town (the local taxpayers) and gown (the college) can be testy.

Alan seemed to be with the town on this one. His area of immediate interest was an overnight bag into which he hastily packed a few things. Alan was making a quick trip to the city to meet with the producers of a new play, which was slated for an Off-Broadway opening in about six months' time. Either Alan had become enough of a name not to need to audition, or they simply knew his work. Given the level of talent attached to the project, lovingly described by his agent, the production team clearly had plans to take this to Broadway. They were opting for an Off-Broadway run that would be successful enough to warrant a move—by popular demand!—to the Great White Way. In this business, as in so many others, marketing was all.

As he packed, Alan listened to what Erica was saying but offered no comment. She had comment enough for both of them, as least as far as this new information was concerned.

"Bee pollen on the stage? How did that get there? Then again, students walk all over campus and could have tracked in the pollen. Given that bees usually fly, it was unlikely that a bee tracked in the pollen on its little bee feet. Maybe the person assigned to sweep the stage that day hadn't done a very good job and left a residue. Then again, Jessa could have been asleep when the bee stung her, and maybe never knew what hit her. But sitting up? How many people can sleep sitting up, leaning on an unforgiving brick wall? And if she were awake at the time of the bee's arrival, why didn't she simply wave it away or remove herself from the area?"

Alan zipped the overnight bag as he said, "Erica, you have managed to keep a safe distance from this thing, and I'm grateful for that. But this is one mystery you cannot solve, because there is no mystery. A tragic death happened under circumstances that haven't been completely explained and maybe never will be. She was in the theater at night. A bee stung her. How did the bee get in? I don't know. But it did. And she died from an unexpectedly severe reaction to a bee sting. Period. Full stop. Case closed."

Erica stared at him and waited until he was finished. He had a little more to say.

"At this point, I don't know what kind of answers would help the family," Alan continued. "Nothing can or will bring her back. They lost their daughter in a freak occurrence, but she is still dead. An *accidental* death. It's a fact of their lives that they have to live with. Especially the sister. Her twin. I can't imagine what she's going through. Rather than asking who shed bee pollen on the stage of the Brink, why not ask yourself how you can help this girl get through the next few months? She's in your class, sitting right there, pouring her heart out whenever you give her the chance. Maybe direct your efforts there."

As she listened, Erica decided that no argument would be the best way to go, especially given the closeness of Alan's train time. She opted for the more politic route.

"You have a point, Alan," Erica replied. "In the midst of all of this drama, that may be the best thing for me to do. I've been trying to meet with her, but she always has somewhere else to be. I'll make sure to get her in my office this week. Now, you better go."

Alan's face reflected his surprise at Erica's lack of push back. A check of his watch confirmed that he had to move or risk missing his train. Lifting the strap of his bag over his shoulder, he gave Erica a quick kiss and promised he would be back the following afternoon. By the time he closed the door, Erica had come to another decision. She would limit any discussion of the "unfortunate accident" with Alan, and find more enthusiastic ears, like those of Tasha or Daphne. And she would meet with Joy this week, no excuses accepted.

Chapter 15

When shall we three meet again?
In thunder, lightning, or in rain?
When the hurlyburly's done,
When the battle's lost and won.
William Shakespeare

The pop-up performances were supposed to have an element of the impromptu, not necessarily in the choice of material, but in terms of when and where they would be staged. And yet, some presentations were more premeditated than others.

Alexis, Ashley, and Ava had chosen *Macbeth*'s three witches as their performance piece, a move that surprised no one. When Shakespeare's witches ask, "When shall we three meet again?" they stir a cauldron bubbling with a nasty brew. These three witches were far from haglike—no ugly sisters here—given that they were dressed in ball gowns left over from last year's production of *Cinderella*, in which Ashley had the title role. They intoned their lines like the cool girls describing a club that everyone would want to join if only they could. Curious how often life imitates art.

It was a production concept that a clever director might borrow someday, and that was not where the cleverness ended. Aside from rifling the wardrobe closet that was off limits to other students, they somehow managed to alert most of the theater faculty to the time and place of their offering, at the center of the quad, where a number of students would be crossing as they moved between classes.

Back from the big city, Alan was in attendance, and Erica had been dragged along.

"Nothing like a little spontaneity to liven up the day," she said, as the performance ended, and the ladies had taken their bows.

"They let it slip in class that this would be happening. The other students took their cue from that," Alan explained.

"And most of the relevant faculty," said Erica. "I saw Cressida with Luke by her side in the front. They would have led the applause at the end—"

"If only Kellan hadn't beaten them to it. Yes, I saw that too," Alan admitted.

"They give 'ugly sister' a whole new meaning," Erica said as they walked away.

From across the retreating crowd, she spotted Joy, who was carrying a load of books and walking in the direction of the library. Erica knew she had to grab her chance, but she would need reinforcements.

"Alan, do you have a minute? I see a student I want you to meet."

"Okay," he said, sounding a little hesitant. This was the first time on this or any campus that she'd offered to introduce a student.

Erica adjusted their route and moved in the direction of Joy's. They soon crossed paths. Forced spontaneity seemed to be the order of the day, so Erica decided to do her bit.

"Joy, hi!" she said. "I thought it was you. Were you at the performance?"

"A text went out last night," Joy answered. "I had a class. Now I have to get these books back to the library before they're overdue."

Working in the Theater Department, Erica had to remind herself that some students actually read books beyond Stanislavsky's *An Actor Prepares* or the memoir by the Broadway diva of the moment. Based on the books she carried, Joy had a daunting reading list, many with titles that Erica could not begin to translate.

The weight of the books seemed to lighten considerably as Joy's attention shifted to Erica's companion. From the look on her face, just shy of star struck, it appeared that Joy had caught Alan in his feature film debut.

"Joy, do you know—"

"Hi," said Joy, smiling at Alan. "I saw you in that movie. You were great."

"Thank you," said Alan, smiling back. Alan had taught her sister, if only for a few weeks, so it was clear who his newest fan was. If Alan were unsettled by the appearance of Jessa's identical twin, he betrayed nothing, his acting training serving him well.

"Would now be a good time to meet?" asked Erica, interrupting the communal grinning. "We could help you take these back to the library, and you and I could have a quick chat. Just to touch base," she added, as nonchalantly as possible.

"Why don't I return these to the library for you?" said Alan. "I have a rehearsal in a few minutes, and I can drop these on the way, if you want. That should save you some time," he said, directing his last comment to Erica.

Erica had brought Alan along as bait and hadn't expected him to do any heavy lifting. She appreciated his assistance nonetheless. He took the books from Joy, who was visibly disappointed that he wouldn't be part of the ensuing conversation. Still, she agreed to the plan with a nod and a quiet "Okay." Their fingers did touch during the handoff, but this would be the extent of Joy's brush with celebrity. It would have to do.

Erica led Joy back to her office at a speedy pace before the magic wore off. They made it there before

Joy came up with another reason why she needed to be elsewhere. Erica didn't think Joy was ducking her exactly. However genuine Joy's excuses were, she still thought it was time for them to talk.

"So, Joy," Erica said, after unlocking the door to her office and both were seated. Conversations tended not to linger in this room, given the minimal level of comfort offered by the standard-issue chairs.

"I'm glad we finally have a chance to talk. How are things going?"

"Professor Duncan, I'm sorry if what I've been writing in class is a little off topic," Joy began. "I don't really have time to read all the plays, but I do like being there. In the class. I'm beginning to see what Jessa liked about the theater."

"It's really not a problem," Erica said. "I appreciate that you always use the play we're discussing as your jumping-off point. And if this is helping you, I'm all for it."

Joy, who had lowered her head for a moment, now raised it with a shy smile.

"It does help," Joy said. "More than talking to a therapist in the Counseling Center. I went there a few times and gave it up."

Erica could have asked why but chose not to go there.

"The theater people are so nice," Joy continued. "So are the people in the Bio Department, but it's different there. We talk about science, not other stuff."

If by other stuff, Joy meant the death of her sister, Erica could see why they would shy away from that topic. She herself referred to it in the most oblique way possible. As Polonius said in *Hamlet*, "By indirections find directions out." Then again, Polonius was almost always wrong.

"You know Kellan, right?"

Erica was initially startled by this jump in the conversation. Retracing her steps, she realized that Joy was still on the topic of "theater people are so nice." Erica simply nodded her agreement.

"I know Kellan from the apiary," she said. "He's such a good listener. I met him last year, when I was a freshman and he was a junior. They make the new beekeepers fill the bottles with honey and label them. Kellan was supervising. We talked as we worked." The memory, as reflected on her face, was obviously a happy one.

"Kellan said that you're not a true beekeeper until you've been stung. I told him I'd never been stung. My sister was, once. Jessa could never be a beekeeper because she was stung as a little kid by a swarm of bees. She was playing too close to a hive near a fuse box at the back of our house. After that, she freaked out whenever she saw anything that even looked like a bee. She would never go anywhere near the apiary on campus. Apiphobia, they call it. Fear of bees."

Erica nodded to show that she was still listening even though her thoughts were elsewhere. Jessa was right to avoid bees at all costs. Being stung as a child could make her sensitive to any future sting, dangerously so, as it turned out. Apparently, Joy thought of allergies as something that made you sneeze, unaware that should her sister be stung again, it could lead to a severe reaction and even more severe consequences. Erica chose not to share this information with Joy. That could wait until another day, and hopefully, another person to impart this knowledge.

Instead, Joy had some information she wanted to share with Erica.

"Jessa told me that she saw you in the theater the first time she tried to see Rosaline." Joy said this in so non-committal a way that it was hard to tell if this was an accusation, a threat, or simply a statement of fact. Erica chose to go with the last.

"Yes," Erica said, "Jessa was not too happy that I woke her up. She decided to try another day, I guess."

"I guess," said Joy in an even tone.

"Did you see her that day?" Erica asked, modelling her tone on Joy's.

"I saw her every day," Joy answered, with more than a hint of annoyance. "I mean I did before..."

An experienced teacher, Erica could tolerate silence for an indefinite period of time, so she let the pause linger until Joy felt the need to fill the void.

"Of course, I was there," Joy said. "No big surprise. She got herself into another situation where she was scared to death, and called me to come over and boost her confidence. Or help her find some. Jessa told me where to meet her, at a back door of the theater that someone had left open. She didn't bother to lock it. If they had some kind of alarm, it was off. Nothing flashed or buzzed when I went in.

"I tried to talk her out of that stupid stunt and get her out of there. Once she settled her nerves, she was hell bent on staying. Nothing I said would change her mind. Of course, I got to walk across campus by myself late at night. Not the best idea. But what was best for me was never a thing with Jessa. My last words to her were 'You're welcome, Jessa.' There was no thank you. She smiled at me and curled up on that pile of rope."

Joy checked the time on her phone, and insisted that she really did have someplace to be. Erica was just as glad. She was about to end their short conversation with "See you in class," when Joy answered the unasked question.

"What is it they say on all those crime shows? She was alive when I left her." Then, after shifting her positon in the chair, Joy insisted, "I could never hurt my sister. It would be like hurting myself." Then, facing Erica with an unwavering stare, she added, "So, Professor Duncan, can I go now? Did you find out what you wanted to know?"

Erica ignored the question and simply said, "You know my door is always open, Joy. Any time you want to talk, about anything, really, feel free to stop by."

"You bet," Joy answered, already halfway out the door. Erica wondered if she would see her again in class, or if Joy had had enough of the theater for now.

Chapter 16

Even bees, the little almsmen of spring bowers,
know there is richest juice in poison-flowers.
John Keats

There were more than bees buzzing around the Canfield campus.

The news had spread like wild fire, if wild fire had a user name and an IP address. The death of Jessa Craven, previously identified as accidental, at least as far as the public was concerned, had been officially deemed deliberate. Everyone knew that an anonymous bee had done it. During the autopsy, the county coroner noticed an indentation at the site of the wound. It was the ring around the bee sting that got his attention. When it swelled, due to Jessa's sensitivity, the rim of what appeared to be a small circular jar, held down with some pressure, left its mark. So the bee had gotten help in locating its target, if stinging Jessa was, in fact, its intent. The current thinking was that the intent belonged to someone else, a person or persons thus far unknown. And that would make it homicide.

When or if this information had been shared with the institution, the college had yet to say. It could have been leaked by the authorities, or the authorities could have sprung an unintentional leak, which found its way to the campus at large. Either way, the speed of the students' communication system was impressive, rivalling that of the bees themselves. Although the bees were not yet online, they were in the air. They could dance their language by angling their bodies to the ceiling of the hive, alerting the other bees to the location of flowers, water, or even a potential new home. The students relied on a more tried and true method, as least for them. They shared whatever they heard on any and all media platforms. Whether true, false, or somewhere in between, word got around.

Erica contemplated this new development as she walked into the student center, heading for the bottomless cup of coffee available to faculty members. Even part-timers could take advantage of this perk, which Erica did, and frequently. Adding low fat milk to the steaming brew, she noticed that Canfield's three leading ladies had seated themselves at a center table. Over the din of utensils scraping plates, they held court, their conversation intentionally overheard by anyone who was nearby and interested. Clearly, they had heard the news. Of course, it started with Alexis.

"Kellan said that he knew her from the apiary and she was totally jealous of her sister. They talked a lot when they were pouring honey into bottles, or whatever it is they do over there."

"Kellan told me that she didn't even want to come here," Ashley added. "Her sister made her because she knew what a good theater program Canfield has."

"A *great* theater program," Alexis replied, speaking directly to Ava. The third member of their trio seemed uninclined to join the fun. The look on Alexis' face made it clear that it was Ava's turn to jump in. Miss your cue at your peril.

"Kellan said that she knew her sister had a bee allergy," Ava said, with decidedly less enthusiasm.

"Jessa was stung by a bee when she was little, and she had a bad reaction. A Bio major would definitely know that a second bee sting could be dangerous," Alexis asserted.

Unless she didn't, thought Erica.

"That's why Jessa never went near the apiary," Ashley continued. "She was scared of bees. But then, she gets stung by a bee. I mean, it's totally creepy."

"I never go near the apiary," said Alexis. "I don't get the appeal."

"How about saving the bees from extinction?" asked Ava.

"Let them fend for themselves," Alexis replied.

"Then what about the honey?" Ava wanted to know.

"Yuck. Never touch the stuff," Alexis answered, brushing off the suggestion as if it were distasteful.

"And Jessa was way cuter than Joy."

Seemingly intended as the *coup de grace*, this final remark by Alexis went too far, leaving her two listeners lost for words. Ava recovered first, saying, "They were twins, Alexis. *Identical* twins. How did you even tell them apart?"

Rarely speechless, Alexis had nothing to add, so she simply shrugged.

And scene, thought Erica, as she left the room.

When Erica walked into her next class, it was clear that the gossip mill had been working overtime. And it was hardly a gentle hum. Joy, once a figure of sympathy, was eyed with suspicion when she raced into the classroom, as she usually did, almost but not quite late, from her sprint across campus. Out of breath, she did not seem to notice the many pairs of eyes that watched her as she dropped her loaded back pack, which landed with a thud, and readied herself for a session with Pirandello. Pirandello wrote plays that were labelled *absurd* before absurdism was invented. As Erica shuffled papers at the front of the room, she thought back to the scene in the student center. Despite the varying degrees of eagerness shown by the participants, all three had played along, but for the sake of what? With Jessa's unexpected departure, the lead in the play was safely back in Alexis' capable hands. Their winning record was intact. So why try to destroy the reputation of the sister of the girl who had died. To what end?

You won, thought Erica. *Get over it.*

But they hadn't, or someone hadn't. Even Joy had quoted Kellan as a source of reliable information. The words "Kellan said" clearly held sway. He was not part of the scene in the student center, but he didn't need to be. His fingerprints were all over it, whether his role was that of author or simply instigator. Erica wondered what Kellan would say about this if anyone asked.

Pirandello's *Henry IV* was the play of the week. A man is diagnosed as mad because he has taken on the identity of Henry IV, the Henry IV who lived in Germany in the eleventh century. Yes, that one. The man argues that he knows he's wearing a mask, but all people wear masks. He insists that if you know you're wearing a mask in your "real" life, you are sane, and if you aren't, you're crazy. Unsurprisingly, the "sane" people surrounding him refuse to accept this theory. As did a number of Erica's students, exasperated by Pirandello's endlessly shifting sense of what's real. To cap off the discussion, Erica had the students write for the last fifteen minutes on the concept of identity as presented in the play. Joy took this as a cue to discuss the concept of identity as it pertained to her.

"Sometimes, I felt like I was defined by my sister. As if the story of my life was a narrative written by someone else. Even if we were twins, we were still two different people with two different identities. I always felt there should be only one me. There is, but it was always a struggle to carve out my own identity. Then I had to fight to hold onto it. I thought our identities would peacefully co-exist for the rest of our lives, but that's not possible now. It's too late to rewrite that story."

On one hand, Erica was impressed by the student's insight. At the same time, she wondered how hard Joy had to wrestle to maintain control over her own identity, and if anyone had been injured in the process. Given Joy's demeanor in class, she doubted that the rumors casting aspersions on their sisterly bond had reached her. Soon enough, they would. It may have been too late for Joy to rewrite the story of her life with Jessa. Erica wondered if someone else was trying to do just that, and, more importantly, why?

The news had reached Alan too, and he was none too pleased.

"I guess you heard," Erica said, when the two met back at the apartment later that day. Based upon the glass that Alan held in his hand, the cocktail hour had begun, and drinks had been served.

"Everyone in the English speaking world has heard. They're translating it for the rest," Alan replied from his perch on the couch. "I don't know where these students get their information—"

"I have no idea what their sources are, but the information, if not the gloss on it, is usually accurate," Erica said, seating herself on the couch while leaving some space between them.

"I don't doubt their accuracy," Alan insisted. "I do have a problem with the fact that there is no dividing line between public and private anymore. The invasion of the family's privacy for our amusement really doesn't do it for me."

"It does make a significant difference if a deliberate action on someone's part resulted in Jessa's death," Erica answered. "We can't put it all on the bee—"

"Of course it makes a difference," Alan said. "And people should know if there's a killer out there, using bees as his or her weapon of choice."

"I think they already do," offered Erica.

"Fine," he snapped. "From then on, it should be handled by the authorities. Not some misguided if well intentioned someone trying to help."

"By that you mean?" Erica asked.

"If the shoe fits," Alan countered. Erica made no reply.

"Or worse still, treating things as if it's a game, an intellectual puzzle," he went on. "A girl died and a family is grieving. Leave it be. Leave them be. Leave the bees alone, come to that."

"My concern is actually for the student, the girl who is still on this campus," said Erica, her anger rising. "Hard as that might be for you to believe."

"Good. Then do what you can do. For her," he answered. "Now even more than before."

Erica had no way of knowing if Joy would be called in for further questioning, as background on the deceased or in a role far more sinister. She also knew that Joy would be a person of interest to her peers long after any interest from the authorities faded.

Once the news was out, calls from the media flooded the college, followed by another flood of calls from concerned parents. Most wanted the bees immediately expelled from Canfield. The administrator in charge of dealing with such matters assured the parents that their offspring were safe, particularly those without bee sting allergies, which accounts for 92% of the general population. What he failed to mention was that 32% of beekeepers, on average, can experience a severe reaction to a bee sting, their proximity to the bees adding to that risk. It had also been established that the deceased never went anywhere near the apiary, but this detail was saved for another day. He did advise parents, in the nicest possible way, to tell their children to stay away from the apiary if they had any concern about being stung. Canfield wanted happy tuition-paying parents. The college would hold the line until further study indicated the need for evicting the buzzing population, at least the ones with wings.

What they didn't count on was the loyalty of the beekeepers. Despite parental warnings, not a one abandoned the hive. As Trent announced at the next class meeting, the beekeepers would remain at their posts. The extinction of the bee population, the bee-pocalypse, as he referred to it, would not happen at Canfield, not on their watch. Trent rarely volunteered anything in class beyond answering to his name when attendance was called. The fact that he was raising his hand to share this information was the most surprising thing about it, especially since no one had asked about the bees or their welfare. Clearly, Trent had found a home. Joy was not in class that day, so she could not reinforce his sentiment. It is unlikely that her support would have made much difference.

Chapter 17

*There's no damn business like show business—you have to
smile to keep from throwing up.*
Billie Holiday

Rehearsals continued apace. It was a tradition in the
Theater Department that anyone who wanted to, could
sit in on rehearsals. This occurred once the production
had gotten to the point of being performed on stage
rather than in a rehearsal room with tape marks on the
floor to show where the scenery would go. Alan
explained to Erica, as it had been explained to him, that
something in the last will and testament of Rosaline
Vander Brink required that the theater be open to
everyone, always. They still locked the doors at night,
allegedly, but rehearsals were open to anyone enrolled
in theater courses. The only prerequisite was that you
could not disturb the action onstage or you would be
asked to leave. Even quiet conversations between
interested parties must be unheard or you would be
unseen in the theater for a very long time. Those
looking to be cast in a production during their four
years at Canfield knew better than to push their luck.

That afternoon, Alan was off working with a couple
of students on their audition pieces, so Erica amused
herself by sliding into the back row of the theater to
check on the progress being made on *Hedda Gabler*.
The production itself was in pretty good shape. Alexis
was center stage, naturally, seated on what would
become an upholstered divan. For now, the divan
consisted of several folding chairs clustered together.

Alexis didn't believe in saving herself for performance and emoted away as Judge Brack, played by a student Erica didn't know, threatened her with ruin. In the play, after a drunken evening, Eilert Lovborg believes that he has lost the career-making manuscript that he wrote under the watchful and encouraging eye of the devoted Thea Elvstead. In fact, Hedda's husband, George Tesman, finds Eilert's manuscript and hands it to Hedda for safekeeping. Good move there, Tesman. Jealous of the emotional connection between Thea and Eilert, and referring to the manuscript as "their child," Hedda burns it. When Eilert returns without the manuscript, thinking he had lost it, he wants to kill himself. Hedda generously supplies him with one of her beloved father's pair of pistols, which she herself enjoys shooting off in the backyard from time to time. Hedda expected Eilert's death to be beautiful, but, as Judge Brack later informs her, it was a messy and desperate affair. Worse than that, at least for Hedda, the police have the gun in their custody, a weapon that Judge Brack recognizes as Hedda's. If he tells what he knows and identifies its owner, Hedda's reputation will be ruined. Armed with this knowledge, the judge makes it clear to Hedda that she is in his power, now and forever. Rather than live this way, Hedda retreats to a small room offstage and, ending the play with a bang, shoots herself with her father's remaining pistol.

Given all the terrible things the character has done, Alexis managed to make Hedda almost sympathetic, which was no mean feat. The student playing Brack, however, an African American student only a little taller than Alexis, would be twisting his mustache if he had one, choosing instead to emphasize the melodrama of the piece. In the front row, Luke, who was directing the play, and Cressida, who was directing Luke, watched carefully. Then, they made comments.

"Nice work," said Luke to Alexis after the scene ended. He looked to Cressida, who nodded her agreement, so all was right with the world, at least as far as the actress playing Hedda was concerned. Judge Brack would not have it so easy.

"Jordan, we need a little less Snidely Whiplash, and a little more realism from Brack. We get that he's the villain, you're doing a great job of making that clear, but we need to see him as a recognizable human being. A corrupt one, definitely, but still a person. Not a cartoon character."

These words came not from Luke, the official director of the play, the one listed in the program, but from Cressida, who was really in charge. Jordan appeared to take her words in his stride, and nodded to show that he understood what she was saying. The two student actors were currently in two different plays, in two different acting universes. It wasn't that Alexis was receiving preferential treatment. She was, in fact, much closer to the mark than Jordan, who would need to find his way there before opening night.

Seated a few rows in front of Erica were a couple of students she did recognize. Their heads close together, Ashley and Kellan appeared to be having a *tete a tete* throughout the rehearsal, although their conversation could be heard only by them. When Alexis left the stage for a moment as the set was changed, Ashley and Kellan, hand in hand, slipped out quietly. Their destination unknown, the two did not appear to be heading to a study group.

Erica was surprised by this comfortable pairing. In the hive, there can be only one queen, but this colony operated with three. Erica would not have guessed that *droit de seigneur* would be the rule in this cluster, more of a *droit de seigneuresse* arrangement. Kellan acted as though he served the ladies, not the reverse.

Apparently, he serviced them as well. If Kellan were romantically linked to any of the queen bees, Erica assumed it to be Alexis, who seemed to rule the world they shared and sit atop its hierarchy. Erica could only wonder where Ava was this afternoon, and if Kellan planned on meeting her later. All for one and one for all?

When Erica saw Alan at home, she got her answer, at least in part. Ava was one of the students that Alan had been working with that afternoon. Although serious drama was not her strong suit, Alan admitted that Ava's Blanche was coming along, or as Blanche would say, "Sometime—there's God—so quickly!" Ava had told him that the spring comedy would be Oscar Wilde's *The Importance of Being Earnest.* She was deciding which part she would play.

"No, she's not playing Earnest," Alan answered when Erica asked.

"Just wondering," Erica replied.

"As you well know, the character of Earnest, I mean, Ernest, doesn't exist. Someone made him up, this misbehaving brother, to cover up another's indiscretions. On the plus side, there are at least three juicy parts for women in this play. There's Cecily, the country girl; Gwendolyn, the city girl; and, of course, Lady Bracknell—"

"Isn't there a tradition of that role being played by a man?" Erica asked.

"Yes," Alan answered, "and that's the part that intrigues Ava the most. All those quotable lines—"

"'Thirty five is a very attractive age. London society is full of women of the very highest birth who have, of their own free will, remained thirty five for years,'" quoted Erica.

"And so on," said Alan.

"Okay, you're the theater guy. Don't they usually have auditions before the play is cast? The cast does not usually cast itself," Erica said.

"Yes, but at Canfield, they go by their own rules," Alan reminded her. "They want to do this play, they have a strong comic actress, and they know they're going to use her. If she would rather play the middle aged lady with all the good lines, so be it. Certainly more interesting than having either of the ingénues on her resume, which would be more typical and not particularly eye catching."

"Too bad for the guy who's good at comedy and might have added Lady B to *his* resume," Erica said. "Since the part is written for a woman but often played by a man, it's almost like Ava is playing what has become a male role. So good for her, I guess. And good for Canfield. They can be traditional and cutting edge at the same time."

Erica paused before adding, "I still think they should have gone through the motions of auditions first."

"I couldn't agree more," said Alan. "And they will, for all the roles. It's just that one will already be cast."

"Only one?" asked Erica as if she were the wide-eyed ingénue.

"Probably more than one," Alan admitted.

"Nothing like open auditions," said Erica. "Except when they're closed."

It was Alan's turn to nod in agreement.

"Here's a thought," Erica said as a new idea occurred to her. "Maybe Kellan will play Gwendolyn and give the theater world a real treat," Erica offered.

"Kellan?"

"You see him as more of a Cecily?" Erica asked.

"What do you see him as?" Alan inquired.

"Funny you should ask," she said.

Chapter 18

The lovely flowers embarrass me,
They make me regret I am not a bee.
Emily Dickinson

The note left in Erica's mailbox in the Theater Department was short and sweet: "Meet us at the apiary at two, if you can. D and I would like you to join us for a walk." It was signed T. Or at least, it looked like a T, the script so small and cramped that only someone with years of experience reading all types of student writing, often masquerading as chicken scrawl, could make it out. Erica assumed the *T* to be Tasha and wondered why her friend had adopted an initialed shorthand in her note, and hadn't simply texted or emailed the invitation.

But Erica was free and game, so she made her way to the apiary. Production in the hives seemed to be slowing down. Seeing no one in their white gowns on their appointed rounds, Erica went to the door of the warehouse and found it locked. She walked around to the windows facing the hive, where she and Daphne had stood while Daphne explained the basics of beekeeping to her. She could see no one inside. The baby beekeepers must be in class, she concluded, their labeling duties waiting for another day.

Checking her watch, Erica saw that she was a few minutes early. She looked down the path that she had trod, expecting to spot Tasha and Daphne coming up the trail. There was no sign of them. On a beautiful fall day, warm by New England standards, she didn't mind the wait. She was enjoying the quiet of the woodsy scene, interrupted only by the rustle of leaves, and thought about nothing. Then, out of the corner of her eye, she thought she saw a long, lean flash of white moving quickly through the trees. Did the beekeepers play hide and seek on a slow day at the hives? Or maybe it was a game of tag, where they chased or were chased by the bees. This continued until another sound broke through the tranquility, a sound that was a little too close for comfort. A bee was buzzing near her, though she in no way resembled a source of nectar. Erica doubted that "I come in peace" would have any meaning for the bee in question. So she stood very still, hoping that he or she would quickly lose interest and fly away.

Unfortunately, he or she brought a friend. More than one. It wasn't exactly a swarm, but it was enough; it would serve to shatter the calm as the bees convened around her. While some find the vibrating hum of bees to be soothing, Erica was not one of those people. As their meeting was called to order, she decided that it was time to move slowly, carefully, to another location. Anywhere but here. She did not want to rattle them, and she had no desire to find out what her tolerance for bee stings might be, never having been stung.

More unfortunately, they weren't going anywhere. As they buzzed and dove around her, Erica considered running but assumed that rapid movement would only encourage a sting. Things began to escalate when a couple of bees landed on her arm. She managed to shake them off before any real harm was done. This was more than a curious bunch of bees, out for an amiable stroll.

Erica decided that the only thing to do was to make a break for it. Her best chance was the warehouse so she ran to the door, hoping that someone had come in while she was fending off her new friends. She got to the door and began to bang on it with one hand as she rattled the knob with the other.

The door was locked until it wasn't.

A figure in white, covered from head to toe in protective gear, opened the door. Erica raced into the warehouse as quickly as she could, given the stickiness of the floor, and exchanged places with the unknown beekeeper, who went out to meet the bees. Armed with the smoker used to calm them, the still unidentified figure moved the bees back in the direction of the hives, a scene that Erica watched from the window. Some of the bees returned home, while others dispersed in search of more amenable targets.

With the mission accomplished, the beekeeper returned to the warehouse. Given the camouflage, Erica had no clue who her savior might be. Once inside, the veiled pith helmet came off, and the beekeeper's identity was revealed. It was Joy, which was exactly what Erica felt upon seeing her.

"Thank you," Erica said, and meant it.

If she had been expecting sympathy from her rescuer, Erica was much mistaken. From Joy's expression, Erica could see where her student thought the blame lay.

"What happened?" Joy asked, making no attempt to mask her irritation.

"Pretty much what you saw," said Erica. "I was waiting for a couple of friends, and for some reason, the bees wanted to make my acquaintance. I am seriously rethinking my choice of perfume."

"Bees are not, by nature, aggressive," Joy said. "You have to give them a reason to attack. By them, I mean the worker bees and the queen. The drones don't have a stinger."

"Good to know," said Erica.

Joy ignored this and went on. "If they think someone is threatening their home, their hive, they react. And when they sting, they release pheromones that get other bees worked up, and they join in."

"I wasn't near the hives, and I didn't get stung. I was standing over there," Erica said, indicating a point at a safe distance from the hives.

"And you didn't agitate the bees?"

"No."

"Or try to raid the hive?"

"With my bare hands? And no protective clothing? Of course not."

"It can happen."

"Maybe if you're a bear looking for lunch. I had no plans to take home a free sample."

"No, that wouldn't make sense," Joy admitted. "Was anyone else around? Anyone threatening the hive?"

"No, the warehouse was locked, and there was no one outside, at least that I saw." Erica chose not to mention the flash of white that may or may not have been a person, who may or may not have been there and meant her harm.

"Oh," said Joy, looking genuinely surprised. "I thought...well, maybe he's late."

"Who is?" asked Erica.

"Just another beekeeper. I thought he'd be here by now."

As they spoke, the door to the warehouse slowly opened. Evidently startled to see them, Trent entered the warehouse. From the look on Joy's face, it was clear that this was not the beekeeper she had in mind. Trent's enthusiastic "Hi, Joy" was met with Joy's more subdued "Hi, Trent." Trent did not seem to notice and followed up his initial greeting with a friendly "Hey, Professor Duncan."

"Hi, Trent," Erica said, then turned to Joy. "Thank you, again," she said. "For your help."

"No problem," Joy replied. "Remember, the bees are our friends until we cross them."

"Isn't that always the way," Erica said as she made her exit.

Chapter 19

How doth the little busy Bee
Improve each shining hour,
And gather honey all the day
From ev'ry op'ning flow'r!
Isaac Watts

Erica shot Tasha a quick email about their missed meeting, which Tasha then forwarded to Daphne. Both replied with profuse apologies. They had been in class at two o'clock, and neither knew anything about the note. The three met up in the late afternoon at one of the less populated coffee shops on campus to discuss who might have left it. Both students and faculty could be included on that list, so discretion was essential.

"I'm so sorry," Tasha said, once they were seated.

"I know, you said in your email," said Erica. "It's not your fault."

"Did you keep the note?" asked Daphne.

"No, I tossed it," Erica said. "I even went back to the mailroom in the department, but the wastebasket had already been emptied. Getting caught rummaging through the trash would probably not do wonders for my reputation."

"True," Tasha agreed.

"I'm not sure how much help a handwriting analysis would be," Erica suggested. "The writing was barely legible. I could only make it out because I've been reading student writing for a while now."

"Well, I'm sorry anyway," Tasha repeated. "If you ever get another mysterious note from me and it says to meet near the hives, forget it. I never go near there."

"You've been stung?" Daphne asked.

"No, and I plan to keep it that way. The bees stay on their side of the campus and I stay on mine," Tasha replied.

"That's probably wise," said Erica. "They gave me kind of an apian welcome, buzzing and diving at me."

"*You* got stung?"

"No, Daphne, but it was an up-close-and-personal experience I don't plan to repeat," Erica answered.

"Did you do anything to upset the hive?" Daphne wanted to know.

"No," Erica said, thinking to herself that Daphne was clearly on the side of the bees. "I stood quietly outside the warehouse, which was locked by the way, or I would have escaped the bees more quickly. A student beekeeper saved me—one I know, in fact. You know Joy...."

Everyone on campus knew Joy. First as the poor girl whose sister died, then as the girl whose sister died thanks to someone with a knowledge of bees. Joy did fall into the latter category, but she was certainly not alone.

The three held an impromptu moment of silence for the deceased before the conversation continued.

"You'd be amazed by the amount of cross-pollination there is among the beekeepers," Daphne began.

"Is that code for something?" Erica asked.

"I was wondering the same thing," said Tasha. "Is there some fertilizing going on?"

"No doubt, and I hope they use protection. But that's not what I mean," Daphne said. "We have people from majors all across the campus, Joy among them. A couple from the Theater Department, in fact. A new student, Trent, is very enthusiastic, and Kellan, of course—"

"Kellan, yes, Kellan, of course," Erica said, with a distinct lack of enthusiasm.

"You know him?" asked Tasha.

"Only from a distance," said Erica. "One I'm happy to keep between us. He does seem to pop up in the most unexpected places."

"He's in my Balinese Theater seminar," Tasha said. "More interested in his three girlfriends than the material I'm discussing, but he's passing the course."

"Are they all his girlfriends? I wondered," Erica said.

"Who are they?" asked Daphne, whose knowledge of theater students extended only to those who found their way to the apiary, which the theater's queen bees had not.

A rundown on the trio quickly followed, and the conversation returned to the queen bees with which Daphne was more familiar.

"Speaking of the poor girl," said Daphne, "the one who died, I mean. There is another detail that hasn't gotten out but will before too long. I overheard a couple of my colleagues talking in our mailroom. Don't ask me how they know. Somebody must know someone in the county coroner's office."

"The only thing they talk about in our mailroom is have you seen the latest Broadway show that got a good review in the *Times*? Everyone is expected to have seen it and to have an opinion," Erica said.

"Or they leave prank notes," said Tasha.

"Yes, that too," Erica admitted.

"Sounds like fun," Daphne said.

"As you were saying...?" Erica asked, trying to get things back on topic.

"Yes, well, usually when a bee stings, the stinger is ripped out of the bee because the stinger is barbed." Daphne explained.

"I'm with you so far," said Erica.

"In this case—"

"The bee didn't die, and it's being brought up on charges?" asked Erica.

"The bee died," Daphne said emphatically. "It's very dead. In fact, it was still attached to the stinger. Or, I should say, she was still attached to the stinger. It was a female."

"A queen?" asked Tasha.

"No, said Daphne. "Queens are definitely female, but so are worker bees. And queens can sting, but their stinger is smooth, unlike the worker bees. The barbed stinger goes in once and stays there, so that's it for the worker bee. It dies. The bee and its stinger are often found in separate pieces, if the bee is found at all. With a smooth stinger, the queen can sting more than once. The thing is, she rarely leaves the hive. The only things she tends to sting are the up and comers, the competition, the baby or virgin queens. Whether they've been hatched or not."

"Okay," Tasha said, making the word sound like more of a question.

"It's a battle to the death in those hives," Erica offered.

"It can be," Daphne agreed. "And it's also weird because of the type of bee that was involved, which has been identified. It was a Russian honey bee."

"So, Russian interference?" asked Tasha.

"More meddling?" Erica wanted to know.

"No," answered Daphne, stretching out the word. "The hives at Canfield don't make use of Russian bees. We use Carniolan honeybees, for a number of reasons."

"There are different kinds of bees? Who knew?" asked Erica.

"Beekeepers," said Daphne, who then explained the difference. "Russian bees are more resistant to mites that can kill the hive, but they can also be more aggressive. They tend not to play well with other strains of bees. Carniolan bees, on the other hand, are good breeders and keep a clean hive. More importantly, they are known to be milder in temperament, which is why we use them with all the students around."

"I must have met a cranky bunch," said Erica. "I would not describe their behavior as kind and gentle."

"If you didn't provoke them, then someone or something did, just in time for your arrival," Daphne reminded her.

"That thought did occur to me," Erica admitted.

"But speaking of cross-pollination," asked Tasha, "couldn't a Russian bee have snuck into the hive undetected? The bees do get around."

"They might," Daphne answered. "Bees are usually bred in southern states because of the warmer climate, and sent up north in a sealed package. Otherwise, it would be one heck of a commute."

"You can get bees by mail?" asked Tasha, visibly horrified by the prospect.

"Yes," said Daphne. "In the small or the economy size. People buy them when they're starting a new hive. The small package would be a queen plus a couple of worker bees to keep her company and feed her. Otherwise, she won't survive because she doesn't feed herself. With three or more bees, it's free shipping. Or you can always buy in bulk. And you better be home when the FedEx guy arrives."

"So you're saying that a Russian bee was deliberately inserted into the hive?" Erica asked.

"Or it was deliberately inserted into the student's leg," Daphne answered. "Remember that circular indentation around the site of the sting. Her leg swelled and there it was. If she didn't have so severe a reaction to the sting, the circle may never have been visible."

"In case the bee attached to her leg wasn't enough to get people's attention," Erica said.

"That would do it," Daphne agreed. "And the bee venom, which is called apitoxin, can pump into the sting site for more than a minute. Even if the bee is dead, or until the stinger is removed."

"Which Jessa's never was," finished Erica.

"Not until it was too late," said Daphne.

"I've had enough of this bee talk," Tasha insisted. "And we're no closer to figuring out who left that note."

"I have no clue," said Erica.

"Maybe it was a prank...but with unexpected consequences?" Tasha volunteered.

"Well, I wasn't stung," Erica replied. "And it may just have been a coincidence that the bees were out when I got there, and no one was in the warehouse." But something about Tasha's suggestion resonated. "*A prank gone wrong*," Erica thought to herself. That was certainly something to consider.

Chapter 20

People don't do such things!
Henrik Ibsen

"Kellan, what the hell?" a female voice said.

Erica overheard this question as she moved between classes. Although she taught her two classes back to back, the registrar's office had scheduled them in two different classrooms in two different buildings. When she called to request a room change, a raspy voice, the veteran of many cigarettes, told her, "Honey, the part-timers get what's left over." The call abruptly ended. While the distance between classrooms made for a nice walk on a fall day, the weather in New England tended to go downhill in the later months of the year. This walk would get more interesting as the semester wore on.

Without even glancing into the room as she passed, Erica heard a second voice, the one that had commandeered an empty classroom. This voice she knew.

"Eilert Lovborg drinks, but you need to remember that he's also a lapsed aristocrat. An upper class drunk is still upper class. What you're giving me is a stage drunk, a barfly, who can barely afford rot gut on a good day.

"If you read the play, Kellan, you know that Eilert and Hedda would sit together on the same sofa in the same room as her father. With Hedda's dad out of earshot, Eilert would share tales of his dissolute lifestyle with Hedda. What really got Hedda's motor running were these scandalous tales of Eilert's behavior.

"Despite being turned on by Eilert, the bad boy, this same Hedda married George Tesman, whom she can't stand, because none of her other suitors were willing to take her on. In her society, you don't want to end up an old maid. Hedda takes the conservative route because she's terrified of scandal, or anything that might besmirch her or her father's name. As you may have noticed, the play is called *Hedda Gabler*, not Hedda Tesman. That's the way she will always think of herself. Her father's daughter, not her husband's wife. Or the mother of his child."

This speaker, easily identified as Cressida McPheers, interrupted her lecture to direct a compliment to another person in the room.

"Nice work, by the way, Alexis. I can really see where you're going with Hedda."

Cressida had a lot to say about the play. Erica wondered why she was the one saying it. Luke was the play's director of record, so why was Cressida working with the two leads? From what little Erica had seen, Luke seemed to have things under control, the production coming together nicely. Were the actors not getting what they needed from their director and requested extra help? Was it possible that these two students had the chair of the department at their beck and call? It seemed unlikely that Kellan would willingly have walked into a reprimand, though Alexis appeared to be doing just fine. Maybe Alexis was unhappy with her co-star's performance and thought he needed a firmer hand. Maybe it was simply a case of what Cressida wants to do, Cressida does.

Or maybe this was just the way things were done in the Theater Department at Canfield College. Erica had seen firsthand that Cressida had no problem providing feedback at an open rehearsal, so scheduling a more private session might be within her purview. Yet, there seemed to be the crossing of a line here, a treading on someone else's turf. Erica planned to run this by Alan, the arbiter of all things theatrical.

The rehearsal continued.

"Okay, let's try it again, Kellan. This time, give me an Eilert who's willing to throw away everything his wealthy family has to offer because, unlike Hedda, he dares to challenge the rules of his society."

"You know something about that," Alexis could be heard saying, presumably to Kellan, as Erica hurried to her next class.

Who's running this show? she said to herself as she reached her destination, took a breath, and walked into her classroom.

Chapter 21

*Theatres are curious places, magician's trick-boxes where the
golden memories of dramatic triumphs linger like nostalgic ghosts,
and where the unexplainable, the fantastic, the tragic, the comic
and the absurd are routine occurrences on and off the stage.
Murders, mayhem, political intrigue, lucrative business, secret
assignations, and, of course, dinner.*
E.A. Bucchianeri

At home that night, rather than go the takeout route
yet again, Alan suggested they eat out, provided that
Erica find the place. She quickly checked with Tasha
and Daphne for recommendations. Tasha came up with
the name of the restaurant where she dined when her
parents came to town, the type of place an assistant
professor can afford only when someone else is paying.
The Canfield Country House was easily the best place
Erica and Alan had dined since their arrival in town, an
opinion shared by a number of people from the college,
whom Erica and Alan recognized even if they didn't
know their names. They were nodded to and they
nodded back as they made their way to a secluded table
for two in the direction of the kitchen, if not actually
outside its door. For a weekday evening, the restaurant
was surprising full, and Erica had no objection to the
distance between themselves and the other diners.

After ordering a carafe of wine (white) and *hors
d'oeuvres* (several), they took turns eating as they
talked. When Erica recounted the events in the
rehearsal room, Alan's surprise was evident.

"That's odd," he said when Erica finished. "Any
production belongs first and foremost to the director.

His or her word is the final one, at least artistically. On the professional stage, you don't get a show off the ground without the money men and women, the producers. Since the college is putting on this show, there really isn't a producer to answer to unless the production goes over budget."

"Would Cressida be considered the producer?" Erica asked.

"Not really," said Alan. "It's her budget but not her money. Obviously, she can have her say as chair of the department, but the director is in charge of a particular show. Luke gets first pick on the shows, and not just because he and Cressida are buddies. He does good work."

"I know that the director's touch is supposed to be invisible," said Erica. "At the same time, it isn't hard to identify the work of a particular director if you've seen more than one of his or her shows. Having seen Cressida in front of an audience, she doesn't strike me as a behind-the-scenes type of gal. More of an on-the-stage, front-and-center type, whatever that stage might be."

"I think you may be right," Alan interjected.

"She's not quite at the point of needing applause the same way the rest of us need oxygen. Though a jolt now and then would seem to be essential to her well being," Erica finished.

"True enough," Alan agreed. "I've worked with that type over the years. They can be brilliant or sink the production. No one else is on the stage, and nothing else matters."

"And yet Cressida is here, not out there treading the boards."

"Well, here is a pretty nice gig. Here, she rules the roost. Out there, in the cold, cruel world, she's one more actress of a certain age with fewer parts to audition for. This is a secure spot, a sinecure if you will. I don't need to explain to you about tenure."

"No," Erica said. "I'm familiar with the concept."

"Though we're no closer to answering your original question," Alan admitted. "I have no idea why she would be working with students beyond the watchful eye of the actual director. Maybe Luke doesn't know. Maybe Luke doesn't mind. Maybe Luke can't mind. Maybe the students asked ever so sweetly and she said yes, despite her own misgivings."

"There was nothing sweet about the lecture Kellan was getting," Erica said. "Among other complaints, it sounded like he still doesn't know his lines."

"That's not good," Alan replied. "He should be off book by now."

"And he's a sloppy drunk. Or that's what he's playing. Cressida insisted upon Eilert being an upper class drunk as opposed to the lower class type."

"I'm not sure what that is," Alan said. "Or what Cressida has in mind there. Drunk is drunk. It's not really a class issue."

"Well, apparently Kellan should connect with the character, at least in one way. I heard Alexis saying that he would know something about a rich boy trashing all the advantages his family could offer."

"I don't know if that's central to who Eilert Lovborg is," said Alan. "He came from respectability and he isn't anymore. More to the point, it's none of my business how he or they approach the character. And I definitely don't care what Kellan gets up to in his free time."

"Well, he's real popular among the beekeepers," Erica said. "Any statement that begins with 'Kellan says' is taken as truth, not only at the apiary but by the queen bees whom you know so well."

"I will keep that in mind," Alan answered. "Now, we should order entrées. The waiter's patience looks to be running thin. What are you in the mood for?"

"The grilled salmon for me," she said. "A good char makes everything better."

"Okay," Alan replied, as he signaled the waiter. "Let's make it two. Sear 'em up."

Chapter 22

He is not worthy of the honey-comb
That shuns the hives because the bees have stings.
William Shakespeare

After the official news broke that Jessa Craven's death by bee had been helped along by person or persons unknown, a long line of students and faculty were called in for questioning. Some had a direct connection to the deceased. Others had a connection to the apiary. And then there were a few, a not so happy few, who had both. At the top of the list was Joy Craven. In a remarkably short time, she had gone from grieving sister to person of a very different kind of interest.

For most, the conversations, handled by campus security, were strictly informational. Like Erica, the campus police learned more about beekeeping than they ever hoped to know. In Joy's case, however, the interview, handled by the local police and attended by her parents, was more direct and directed. Although the words *means, motive,* and *opportunity* were never spoken, the subtext was clear. Joy confirmed her whereabouts on the evening in question, freely admitting that she had seen her sister in the theater the night Jessa died. As her parents nodded in agreement, she explained how frequently she offered moral support to her sister. When Jessa had bitten off more than she could chew, even a stunt like this, one that her sister had tried to convince her was pointless, Joy was called in to help. And yes, Joy was a beekeeper and not at all intimidated by the buzzing population on the Canfield campus. Motive would be a sticking point, however. Jealousy would be an obvious place to start, but the sisters had opposite areas of interest and separate arenas in which to excel. Jessa and Joy were known to get along, a point confirmed by the resident assistant on their floor in the dorm, reconfirmed by the other students who lived there, and pretty much anyone who knew them. On the question of motive, the questioners would have to wait and see.

According to the college grapevine, Joy handled herself well during the interview. Still, Joy's parents, having been assured that hiring a lawyer would be premature at this point, began dialing as soon as they left the station house.

Daphne had also been called in, which she reported to Erica and Tasha not long after the interview had taken place. Her conversation was on campus with the head of security, Mr. Evans, a retired police officer with decades of experience on the Canfield force. Daphne described his manner as kind but professional.

"He's an old hand at this," she began. "He made it clear that we are compatriots in the fight for justice. Then, he trotted out some practiced exasperation along the lines of 'these kids today' to see how I would react. He seems to think there's a line on campus between students and faculty."

"He's not wrong there," said Erica. "Though I don't think it has to be adversarial."

"There should be some kind of line," Tasha insisted. "Separate entities, but not necessarily opposing. With different jobs to do and different lives to live."

"Agreed," Erica said. "So let's get down to the nitty gritty. What did he ask?"

"You mean, after my name, rank, and serial number?" Daphne began. "He wanted to know about the inner workings of the apiary. As someone who's there in a supervisory capacity, I should know. How much access do students have? What are they allowed to do there? Are there regulated hours? Do they have a key to the warehouse? All sorts of questions about the running of the place."

"So, strictly background," Erica said.

"Mostly," Daphne replied. "He seemed very interested in where our bees come from, and how we get them. I explained to him about ordering bees online, and he had much the same reaction you two did. He was surprised to learn that you can get them delivered."

"You can get anything delivered," Erica said. "I didn't know that included overnighting a packet of bees."

"He seemed particularly interested in queen bees," Daphne added.

"Anyone in particular?" Tasha asked.

"Or the one they found in Jessa's leg?" Erica asked, a little more bluntly.

"That was a worker bee," Daphne reminded her. "He also mentioned that Jessa had been found seated near the coil of rope."

"Nothing new there," said Erica. "Everybody heard about the rope."

"It wasn't that," Daphne replied. "She was *seated,* leaning against the wall."

"Still no surprise," Erica insisted. "She was on the stage left side. There is no exit stage left."

"No, that's not it," Daphne said, a little more emphatically.

"Maybe if you let her finish," Tasha tactfully proposed.

Erica took her cue and said nothing, leaving room for Daphne to add, "Sitting up after a bee sting is the worst thing you can do. It's called the fatal posture. Sometimes when people are stung, they sit up to take the stinger out, if they can reach it. I guess it's a natural enough reaction. Sitting up after a bee sting, or moving to any upright position, can be dangerous for someone at risk of anaphylactic shock, which is all of us until we know how well we tolerate a sting. A person in shock, for any reason, will usually lay down. Without getting too technical, the blood flow to the heart can stop if this person gets up or sits up, and all the Epipens in the world won't make an iota of difference. The best thing to do is to stay down but raise the legs a little to keep the circulation going."

Erica listened carefully before admitting, "Jessa was sleeping in the theater that night with hopes of seeing the theater's ghost, Rosaline. Don't ask," she said to Daphne, who clearly wanted to.

"I'll explain later," Tasha promised a confused looking Daphne.

Erica continued. "According to the theater grapevine, all the lights were out, even the work light on the stage that usually stays on all night. So Jessa was in the dark. And presumably asleep. If she felt the sting, she might have bolted upright. If she did, why didn't she try to take the stinger out? It was dark, yes. Then again, our students are never without their phones. She could have used that light to see. Or even to call her sister. But she sits up and then just stays there? If she were able to sit upright, it's surprising she didn't do anything to help herself."

The three were silent for a moment, until Tasha offered an explanation.

"Maybe she couldn't pull herself up," she said. "The speed of the bee venom spreading through her system, combined with the fact that she didn't fully realize what was happening to her." Tasha hesitated before taking her argument to its logical conclusion. "Or maybe someone did it for her, pulling her up and leaving her there, leaning on the wall."

"Which would speed up her demise," Erica said.

"But why?" asked Daphne.

"That is always the question," Erica said, asking herself, if not her friends, *I wonder if she saw and knew her killer.*

Chapter 23

*That which is not good for the bee-hive
cannot be good for the bees.*
Marcus Aurelius

It had to happen. Given the cross-pollination between the Theater Department and the apiary, someone had to find the bee-friendliest passage in all of Shakespeare and use it for a pop-up performance. These performances were becoming less spontaneous if people knew where and when to be, but the performers wanted an audience, and an audience they would have. Alan received the text telling him the time and place. Interestingly, Erica did not. And while Erica had described what happened the last time she visited the apiary, he insisted that she come. This might be the one she wouldn't want to miss.

The invitation stipulated that people could watch the performance from behind the window inside the warehouse or on the ground outside. Alan chose the great outdoors. Erica chose the warehouse. As she made her way to the window, amid some gentle jostling from other indoor audience members, she noticed that the floor was just as sticky as it had been on her previous visit, if not more so. As soon as she took her place by the window, she saw that the beekeepers were lining up behind the hives, dressed from head to toe in their protective suits. The tallest speaker was at the center of the line, with the others on either side by order of descending height. Once assembled, they began the speech from *Henry V* that describes how a well-order society is supposed to work:

> Therefore doth heaven divide
> The state of man in diverse functions,
> Setting endeavor in continual motion,
> To which is fixèd as an aim or butt
> Obedience; for so work the honeybees,
> Creatures that by a rule in nature teach
> The act of order to a peopled kingdom.
> They have a king and officers of sorts,
> Where some like magistrates correct at home,
> Others like merchants venture trade abroad,
> Others like soldiers armèd in their stings
> Make boot upon the summer's velvet buds,
> Which pillage they with merry march bring home
> To the tent royal of their emperor,
> Who, busied in his majesty, surveys
> The singing masons building roofs of gold,
> The civil citizens kneading up the honey,
> The poor mechanic porters crowding in
> Their heavy burdens at his narrow gate,
> The sad-eyed justice with his surly hum
> Delivering o'er to executors pale
> The lazy yawning drone.

Erica had no idea whose inspiration this had been or who was performing it, given that it was spoken not by one but by many speakers, reciting the speech as a chorus. The rest of the performance pieces had been suspended after the untimely death of Jessa Craven. No one expected that performance art would be hazardous duty. While Canfield was a selective school, with more eager applicants to choose from, the administration believed—and who could blame them—that they should not risk losing any more of the current population. Those who had not enacted their performance piece would have to write a paper describing what might have been, a performance lost to the ages. He who hesitates is lost.

And yet, this show went on. Choral speaking had not really been in style since the plays of the ancient Greeks, when a group speaking for the common man chanted and moved in unison. Sometimes they posed the questions that the audience would ask the characters if they could. The Greek chorus was led by a *choragos,* the chorus leader, who had the honor of speaking directly to the hero of the play, who enjoyed an elevated position in society, at least until his tragic fall. The anonymous chorus of beekeepers did surprisingly well, even with the buzzing background noise provided by a few of the performers, unless the bees themselves had been corralled into service. With their heads covered by hat and veil, dressed up in their beekeeping best, the students spoke together and could be understood. It was a long speech and all had memorized it, or so it seemed. Instead of droning on, they managed to give it some life. It was about bees, after all.

When the performance ended and the beekeepers lifted their veils, and then took off their hats, it became clear who was who. Erica recognized Trent and Joy, standing at opposite ends of the line, plus a few students from her sections of Introduction to Theater, who had filled out the procession. There were several more she didn't know. At the center of the line, the tallest member of the chorus and clearly their leader, was Kellan, whom the other members of the troupe acknowledged at the curtain call. Applause was led by Cressida and Luke, who braved the outdoors for an up-close view. There was no way of knowing whether Luke had forgiven, forgotten, or simply didn't know that Cressida had been working with selected members of his cast. The three ladies Kellan served were also in attendance, clapping wildly for their friend. Alexis was the most aggressive in her applause, closely followed by Ashley, with Ava the least enthusiastic of the trio. Erica wondered if the three queens were really three of a kind. Still, Kellan had to be given his due. Instead of dividing the speech into sections, giving each beekeeper only a few lines to learn, Kellan had gotten the whole group to memorize the whole thing. His ability to lead, or at least to gain followers, could not be denied. As she and Alan walked back to their side of the campus, Erica wondered if this were the good news or the bad news.

They were silent, deep in their own thoughts. Erica was thinking about what had been said in the speech, while Alan focused on how. There was not much to say about the performance, beyond the originality of the setting.

"So," said Alan, "a bunch of kids lined up behind beehives reciting Shakespeare."

"Yes," said Erica. "They really do break the mold around here when it comes to originality."

"At least you could hear them," Alan admitted.

"More than that, you could make out what they were saying," Erica replied. "Even above the sound of some of them droning, I mean, imitating the sound of bees, while the rest were speaking the speech."

"Could have done without the buzzing," Alan said.

"Agreed," said Erica, wondering if this had been Kellan's idea or if he received outside help. The performance pieces were supposed to be entirely the work of students. After the off-the-record rehearsal led by the department chair, Erica doubted whether Cressida would be willing to make a house call for this type of project, even if requested by Kellan or a member of his cadre.

"And there were very few of them I recognized," Alan said. "Beyond Kellan, of course. And wasn't that—"

"Joy. Yes, that was Joy. She's sitting in on my intro class, as you know, but I think her first allegiance is to the bees. I knew a few others from the same class. So that would make them beginners as far as the theater goes, not yet ready for the rarified air of the advanced acting class that you teach. Either that, or they are just happy to sing the praises of bees when the opportunity presents itself."

"I could make out the words," Alan said, "but I don't know that speech. *Henry V,* isn't it?"

"It's not exactly on the list of Shakespeare's greatest hits," Erica replied. "The Archbishop of Canterbury is explaining to King Henry that he can go off and fight wars—attacking France, of course—while still keeping the peace at home, which is probably just what Henry wanted to hear. And it's true that we can learn a lot from bees, 'creatures that by a rule of nature teach.' It's also true that some bees in a well-ordered hive 'venture abroad' while others work from home. It's just that the speech refers to the hive having 'a king and officers, of sorts' when the hive actually has a queen. And the drones have no stingers. So they would be 'officers' without weapons, and what officer is unarmed? The drones are the first to be ousted if there is a food shortage, so maybe there's some truth to delivering the 'lazy, yawning drone' to the executioner. Despite the fact that we've come to associate their name with sloth, drones aren't entirely lazy, although the worker bees would be the ones to win employee of the month. Drones do what they do in the hive, primarily by doing their service to the queen so that she can bring little baby bees into the world. Only female bees can sting, so that might make them the officers, but in the speech, we're centuries away from women in the military."

"So glad I asked," Alan said, when she took a breath. "So Shakespeare wasn't a beekeeper. Where did *you* come across all this bee lore?"

"Well, the speech I knew before," said Erica. "The life of a drone was new to me until I came to Canfield. You tend to pick it up being around this campus, what with all the bee aficionados here."

"Well, you know what they say about a little knowledge," Alan continued. "Just be careful you don't get stung."

"Trying not to," said Erica.

"Although getting buzzed might be a good idea," Alan proposed.

"I did that already," Erica replied.

"I meant in a good way," he said.

"As in 'a jug of wine and thou'?" she asked.

"Exactly," he said.

"I'm in," she said, as they turned for home.

Chapter 24

To lose one parent, Mr. Worthing, may be regarded as a
misfortune; to lose both looks like carelessness.
Oscar Wilde

Ava Levitan sat alone on a bench near the center of the quad, intently reading. She didn't appear to be waiting for anyone, nor was she accompanied by her usual cohort. Erica passed her as she travelled from her last class of the day to the library, where she planned to grade essays in the relative quiet she would find there. Perhaps Ava's friends were in class, or possibly in rehearsal. Either way, Erica doubled back to seize this rare opportunity. Ava appeared to be the weak link, the least eager of the three when it came to group activities like destroying the reputation of someone they barely knew, just for the fun of it. As she neared the bench, Erica saw that Ava was reading a paperback copy of *The Importance of Being Earnest*, the comedy in which she would undoubtedly star once the casting notice went up.

Given that they had never formally met, anything beyond a friendly hello might seem a little odd. Given Ava's choice of reading material, Erica relied on the tried and true. When speaking to a child, their interests are your interests or it's going to be a very short conversation. Erica expected this would work with millennials too.

"I love that play," Erica said, as she approached the bench, close enough to pretend that she had just read the title.

"Me too," said Ava, looking up. "I've never read it before."

Erica thought this a shocking lapse in her dramatic education but chose not to mention it.

"And there are good parts in it for women," Erica added, sticking to topics that might interest the student.

"I know," Ava replied. "We're doing it in the spring. I play, I mean, I plan to audition for Lady Bracknell."

Erica had hit the sweet spot and took a seat on the bench. Up close she could see that Ava's auburn hair and hazel eyes would certainly qualify her for an ingénue role, yet she chose to play the old lady instead.

"Wow, that's a great part! It's been played by men in recent years. It really should be played by a talented actress. Which I hear you are."

"Thanks," said Ava, looking genuinely pleased. "I appreciate that. Did Alan tell you?"

Erica remembered that Ava was enrolled in the advanced acting class, and that the queen bees had taken Alan out for coffee on the first day to give him the lay of the land in the Canfield Theater Department. What Erica didn't know was that they were all on a first-name basis, a detail she would take up with him later. For now, she introduced herself, without offering a first-name option.

"I'm Professor Duncan," Erica said.

"I know," Ava replied. "Alan's really a good teacher. And coach."

"Good to hear," said Erica. Another detail she would share with him.

"He's helped me a lot on my audition piece for graduate school. The comedy I can do, and the song I can fake. I needed more work on the dramatic piece. I'm doing Blanche from *Streetcar*," she said, as if this were an original choice.

"Really," said Erica, serving up her own piece of acting in pretended ignorance. "Well, I wish you the best of luck. Or break a leg. Whichever works."

"Thanks again," Ava said, and her thanks seemed to be sincere. "I hear Alan is up for a part in an Off-Broadway play."

"Yes," was all that Erica chose to say, smiling as she said it. While Alan's role had not yet been secured, his being in the running was enough for Ava to be suitably impressed.

Where these students got their information was a question still unanswered. She doubted that Alan had shared this with the group. She also knew that he offered anecdotes from his life in the theater, particularly when it came to auditions. He wanted his students to have some sense of what awaited them in the acting world outside the four walls of the Brink, the place where they played, in every sense of the word, for their four years at Canfield. In the real world, it would be work. Stories from the front were, in part, what the college was paying him for.

"So, it's graduate school for you next year," said Erica. "Where are you applying?"

Ava reeled off the names of the most prestigious graduate acting programs in the country, plus a couple in London, thrown in for good measure. There was no identifiable back-up plan. It was top of the line or nothing.

"Wow, that's an impressive list," Erica said. "I hope you get what you want."

"I do too," Ava replied, before adding, "I can't believe it's almost here. I mean, we're graduating next May. It went by so fast."

"It always does," Erica agreed. "It seems like you've gotten a lot of acting experience while you were here.

That should hold you in good stead. And you made some good friends."

Ava looked at Erica and said, "That's true. But we've got to get through this year first." She paused before continuing. When she did, it sounded more like thinking out than talking to the person seated beside her. "Sometimes you just don't know about people. Even people that you think you know well. What they are willing to do, and why they are willing to do it. Even what they're capable of."

Erica was fairly certain that Ava was not talking about the range of her friends' acting ability, but said nothing, waiting for her to continue.

"Sorry, I'm rambling," Ava said, brushing away a curl that had fallen over her eye.

"Not at all," said Erica. "Sometimes the friends you thought you would know forever depart into their own lives. Maybe it's due to distance or a lack of shared interests, or maybe a lack of shared values. Old friends may disappear. There are always new ones to be made."

But not just yet. While Ava listened intently to her words, Erica could see out of the corner of her eye a pair of students approaching them. One tall and the other about a foot shorter, with a crop of bleached blonde hair. As Kellan and Ashley walked up to the bench, Erica noticed that they were not quite hand in hand, but the little fingers of their respective right and left hands were intertwined. Clearly, they were a couple of some kind, possibly with their own secret handshake. Once they saw that Ava was not alone on the bench, they stepped apart, deliberately creating a distance between them, a maneuver that Ava missed as they moved in behind her.

"Hey, Avy," Kellan began, once they were near enough to be heard without needing to shout. "Alexis wants us all in the rehearsal room. She wants you and Ashley to watch us run our lines for *Hedda*."

"Why does she need an audience if you're just running lines?" Ava asked as she turned to him, visibly annoyed. "That's not even a real rehearsal."

"I don't mean run lines," said Kellan, evidently surprised by any pushback to a request from Alexis, whose demands were usually met without question. This was something new.

"I meant practice our scene for acting class. All of us need to be in the rehearsal room. *Now*. Oh, hi, Professor Duncan," Kellan quickly added, as if Erica had just materialized.

"Kellan," Erica said coolly. "And Ashley?" she asked the girl who had stood silently throughout Kellan's speech.

"Yeah, hi," Ashley replied, grinning at Erica, before quickly shifting gears. "*Come on*," she said, trying to cajole her friend into doing something that Ava clearly didn't want to do. "It won't take that long."

Ashley needn't have bothered. Churning across campus in the direction of the bench, like a ship in full sail, came Alexis. Even from a distance and without saying a word, she conveyed the fact that she was not happy. Maybe this is what acting was all about. When she reached the bench, the words came tumbling out.

"What is it with you guys?" Alexis began. "I only have the rehearsal room for an hour. We're wasting valuable time while you sit here. I don't want to look bad in front of—"

Alexis stopped herself when she saw that the last member of the group was not another student. It was, in fact, the person who could easily fill in the name that was missing from this sentence, given that she lived with him.

The gang's all here thought Erica, saying instead, "Alexis," and nodding at her as if they were actual acquaintances instead of two people whose reputations preceded them. Alexis smiled her best innocent smile and said nothing.

"So, Avy, shall we go?" asked Kellan, who bent awkwardly from the waist as he offered Ava his arm. Ava looked as if she would rather hack hers off at the elbow than give it to Kellan. She ignored his gesture and rose under her own steam. Turning to Erica, she said, "It was nice to meet you."

"You too," Erica replied, watching as the student put the paperback into her bag and rejoined the group, who left without good byes. As they retraced their steps to the rehearsal room, Erica noticed that Kellan had his arm around Alexis' waist, with Ashley on the outskirts of the group. Ava walked between Ashley and the couple. All four stared straight ahead. No one was speaking.

Erica was a little surprised by the lack of multitasking on Kellan's part. After all, he did have two hands and could had held onto at least two of the trio as they walked. Ava was the odd woman out here, excluded from a roundelay she apparently had no interest in joining. Erica liked her all the better for it.

Chapter 25

Brothers and sisters are as close as hands and feet.
Vietnamese Proverb

Trent had asked for a few minutes at the start of class to make an announcement. Since Trent rarely said anything in class, Erica agreed but stopped short of letting him distribute fliers. This could lead to a flood of leaflets papering the floor, making more work for the custodians. Given that some students left behind the handouts needed for her class, she doubted that Trent would have much luck connecting with his peers on paper.

"Bee Strong. Bee Proud. Be a Beekeeper," Trent began. His opening did not get the attention of his audience, who were still settling down when he started to speak. "I'm here to talk to you about being a beekeeper at Canfield. It's a great way to meet people on campus."

"Not to mention bees," said a helpful male voice from the back, which Erica did not, at first, recognize.

"That too," said Trent, who seemed to miss the fact that he was being mocked. "I've learned so much about bees and beekeeping since I started to work at the apiary, which most people call the hives. You get to know a lot about bees and the people who work with them. We're looking for a few good people to join us."

Trent stopped to look around the room. There were no takers. He pressed on.

"I have some fliers, if you're interested. You can pick one up after class. I wanted to give the beekeepers armbands to wear with bees on them, but some people thought that was too—"

"Fascist?" offered the same helpful voice. Reading the expression on Trent's face, Erica could see that Trent was uncertain about the word's meaning, but he could tell it wasn't good. Still, Trent would stand up for the bees no matter what.

"What have you got against bees?" the young beekeeper asked, swiveling himself in the direction of the speaker.

"Nothing," said the voice. "And I'd like to keep it that way."

Erica could now identify the other voice. He was an upperclassman enrolled in a course primarily intended for freshmen. Either he was a transfer student making up credits or he had waited until the very last minute to fulfill a requirement. Either way, he wasn't much fun to have around, although he had not quite achieved the level of toxic presence in the classroom. Erica was about to shut down his commentary when a late arrival silenced him and the rest of the class.

Looking a little thinner and a lot paler, Joy raced into the room. Since her interview with the police, she had been keeping a low profile but remained a hot topic on campus. The gossip, as usual, was rife with misinformation. Rumor had it that she left school, either by her own choice or at the request of the college. Allegedly, she was considered a person of interest by the police, though that was hardly grounds for an early departure. Yet here she was, which might quell that rumor at least.

While twenty-five pairs of eyes stared at her, only Trent looked glad to see her, as he motioned her to sit in an empty seat by him. For once, she looked glad to see him and gave him a small but grateful smile as she sat down. *Those beekeepers stick together*, Erica thought, as she moved to a completely different topic, her topic of the day.

"We talked last time about the family dynamics in O'Neill's *Long Day's Journey into Night*. The Tyrones were a fun bunch, with a drug addicted mother, a father and older brother who drink to excess, and a younger brother who is coughing up his lungs due to what his mother insists is only a 'summer cold' but is really tuberculosis, known then as consumption. In the nineteenth century, consumption was considered fatal. The older Tyrones, the parents, operate, for the most part, according to nineteenth century ideas. In the early twentieth century, with decent treatment, a person could survive the disease, as O'Neill himself did. It was at the sanitarium where he recovered that O'Neill decided to get serious about his life and his writing. What I want to look at today is the section in the last act, when the older brother, Jamie, who has been out drinking at a bar, comes home to confront his younger brother and set him straight about their relationship."

Erica asked for volunteers, and two students read the scene in which Jamie insists he's telling Edmund the truth because "I love you more than I hate you." Jamie admits that he has been jealous of his brother since Edmund was born. He hated Edmund because his mother taking morphine for the pain of his brother's birth led to her addiction. Erica reminded the students that Jamie purposely encouraged his younger brother to follow the same paths of dissipation that he had, not because he was looking out for Edmund or introducing him to the ways of his world. He wanted Edmund to fail in life as he has done. At the same time, Jamie is strangely proud of Edmund's achievements, insisting, rightly, that he had more to do with his brother's upbringing than their parents, saying, "Why shouldn't I be proud?...you're more than my brother. I made you! You're my Frankenstein."

Once Erica finished her explanation, she paused and asked, "Who is Frankenstein?"

"The monster!" several students shouted at once.

"Really?" Erica asked.

"Everyone knows that," smirked the student at the back, whom Erica now remembered was named Matt.

"Well, then everyone is wrong," Erica stated calmly, looking in his direction. An upperclassman with attitude could take, and needed, some correcting. A younger student would have received a much gentler approach.

"Actually," said a voice that the class was hearing for the second time that day, "Frankenstein is the name of the doctor, not the monster. The monster was created by Dr. Frankenstein." As an aside, he added, "I saw the movie *Young Frankenstein*, so I know."

"Me too," said a chorus of voices.

"Thank you, Trent. Yes. The monster may be known as Frankenstein, but he's really the Frankenstein monster, or the creature, with no actual name. Sometimes, when a mistake is made often enough, it becomes common usage, no longer an error but instead revealing its own kind of truth. If only in showing how easily we forgive our own faults."

Erica paused for a moment to see if the class was following her. They seemed to be right there with her.

"In making this common mistake, and in taking Edmund for the monster, Jamie is revealing his own kind of truth, one he doesn't realize. From the time of his birth, Edmund has deflected their mother's attention from Jamie, who needs it even more than their father. We've talked about how Tyrone Senior competes for Mary's attention as if he were another sibling—and he usually wins. The mother's attention is in short supply when she is under the influence of drugs. So Edmund simply has to be in order to have an effect on his older brother. While Edmund may be the mother's admitted favorite, Jamie is more his mother's son than his sickly brother. Like his mother, Jamie has an addictive personality, well on his way to alcoholism. His cure, which would be to give up drinking, is emotionally tied to hers, and her cure is failing."

So far, so good, Erica thought as she scanned the room.

"At first, Edmund treats Jamie's statement as a joke: 'All right, I'm your Frankenstein. So let's have a drink.' True to their roles in life, Jamie is the actor and Edmund simply watches. He offers only a few objections to his brother's lengthy harangue, which may do more harm to the speaker than the intended victim. Given Jamie's degree of self-loathing, Jamie may have been the target all along. True to form, Edmund is the passive resister. He allows Jamie to continue his emotionally self-destructive ways with minimal interference.

"Yet the blame for what has become of Jamie cannot be laid entirely at Edmund's door. Edmund may have helped to create Jamie, to make him what he is, but Jamie is an active participant in his own life. Jamie has become the Frankenstein he intended Edmund to be, and which Edmund, in fact, is. They've always been 'more than brothers,' and now they are one and the same, Frankensteins, both creator and monster, in every sense of the word."

While some students scribbled furiously to get all of this down—it might be on the test!—others simply watched. A few stared into space, reflecting the range of grades that would follow at the end of the semester. Having said enough, Erica turned to the class to bring them into the discussion.

"Sibling relationships can be complicated. The Tyrone brothers are ten years apart in age—and still living at home, I might add. They are also very close, supposedly best friends. Jamie may be losing his only friend in telling Edmund the truth, but are there any signs of hope in what Jamie has to say to his brother?"

"Jamie says it *because* he 'loves him more than he hates' him," said one of the furious scribblers. "He warns his brother to watch out for him once Edmund gets out of the sanitarium. Jamie will be there, pretending to be his friend, but ready to stab him in the back. Doesn't he say something about saving his brother?"

"'Greater love hath no man than this, that he saveth his brother from himself,'" Joy volunteered.

The source of the quotation startled the class, who looked in her direction for a reason beyond the mere fact of her presence. Joy tended to watch intently but rarely participated in discussions. Still, it was nice to know that in her time away from class, she was doing the reading.

"Good recall, Joy," Erica said, acknowledging the student's contribution as she redirected the class's attention.

"What else can we say about the brothers' relationship? And for every word you use to describe it, you need to come up with a specific example to support your idea. If you say it's *complicated*—and what relationship isn't?—then you have to come up with an example of a complication. Actually the word *complicated* may keep us busy for a while. The complications abound in the Tyrone family."

Erica looked around the room.

"Why don't we start with . . . Matt."

Matt looked up, clearly surprised that he was being called on. Erica thought that with all the words out there, he might redeem himself after making the common mistake about Frankenstein.

"My word would be 'complicated,'" Matt said. "Jamie says he loves and hates his brother at the same time."

Maybe not, thought Erica.

"True, Matt, but we already covered that. Can you think of another example of love and hate at the same time?"

"My brother and I usually get along. Sometimes we fight," he offered.

"Okay, but we're talking about the Tyrone brothers. Can you think of an example in the play that would follow this pattern?"

Reading the play would be essential to coming up with an answer, so Matt could not. After a short pause, Erica decided to move things along. She said, "You think about that and we'll get back to you. Does anyone else have an example, or a new word to use?"

Erica's interaction with Matt had convinced the class that the real topic of discussion was their own relationship to their siblings. They would have reached this conclusion in any case. Any discussion of literature was really an opportunity to talk about themselves. It was Erica's job to work in the play now and then.

Students came up with a variety of suggestions. The brothers were loyal; they always split whatever money they might have, usually doled out by their father. At the same time, they made fun of their father and his cheapness, the result of an impoverished childhood. They called him a miser, so cheap, he'd rather stumble around in the dark than keep a single light bulb burning. They were devoted to their mother, the only woman to whom Jamie had ever been faithful, "in his fashion."

"They fight too," Matt said, as he abruptly rejoined the conversation. "After Jamie says that Shakespeare thing, Edmund hit him." A few titters could be heard from various corners of the room.

Erica knew which scene he meant but required a more complete answer, even from Matt. Doing her best imitation of a patient teacher, she said, "There are many references to Shakespeare in the play. It's a language that all the characters, with the possible exception of Mary, speak and understand. Which example did you have in mind?"

It appeared that Matt had read beyond the opening inscription. O'Neill dedicated the play to his third wife, Carlotta, admitting that the play had been "written in tears and blood." Unfortunately, Matt could not come up with the relevant example. In its way, this was a step forward for the student, though he still needed help to finish his thought. Erica opened it up to the floor.

"Does anyone remember the quotation Matt is referring to?"

The first to answer was Joy: "'The Mad Scene. Exit Ophelia,'" she intoned. "Jamie says it as Mary is coming down the stairs, dragging her wedding gown. She's so far gone that she's living in the past. By the end, Mary thinks that she's a young girl back at the convent school, with her whole life ahead of her."

Her explanation was monotone in its delivery but right on point.

"Yes, Joy, thank you. That's the one," said Erica. Even Matt seemed to offer a reluctant nod. Checking the clock, Erica could see that time was moving toward the end of the hour. The class might be ripe for a short writing assignment. Within siblings on their mind, Erica asked them to pick out one word that described the Brothers Tyrone and expand on the discussion, beyond what had been said in class.

"You can come up with your own word or use one we talked about in class. Remember, you need to look at the play to find evidence to support your claim. You have the play right in front of you. Well, most of you do. And you're writing about the characters in the play, not about yourself and your relationship with a sibling."

"What if you're an only child?" one student asked.

"You're writing about the play, not about yourself," Erica said with some finality. "Are there any other questions?" There were not. Most of the class, Joy included, were already digging into the text to find the answers they were seeking. Or so it seemed.

Erica had asked the question as much to check in on Joy as to check the class' progress. Joy's answer did not disappoint. She did not throw caution to the wind, but her interview with the police hadn't restrained her honesty when discussing her sister.

"I kind of get what Jamie is saying," her answer began. "He says that he loves and hates his brother. Loves him more than hates him, which is why he's saying what he does at the end of the play. He's telling the truth about how he feels by warning his brother to watch out for him when he gets well. It's a weird combination of feelings. Not really in balance or in equal amounts. Sometimes one, then the other. Like being on a seesaw that can make you dizzy.

"I loved my sister, and anyone who says I didn't is lying. I relied on her, and she relied on me. Maybe too much. She was heavy lifting sometimes. She needed a lot of emotional support. Sometimes I resented her for it. And I'm not saying it was all about Jessa, or that it was even her fault. That word you used in class to talk about shared guilt—complicit. I let her do it. I didn't stop her and neither did my parents. But that's another story."

Joy had stopped there, which was just as well. In the current climate, even admitting to ambivalent feelings about her sister could be a problem for Joy. Erica sometimes returned the students' in-class writing with comments, sometimes she read them and kept them. She decided to hold onto these for a while, with Joy's answer receiving special attention. Whether in an abundance of caution or simply in a protective mode, after crumpling the page, Erica tossed it in the trash. Joy needed all the help she could get.

Chapter 26

Opening Night: The night before the play is ready to open.
George Jean Nathan

The semester rolled on, as semesters do. The date of the first major production of the theatrical season, the highly anticipated *Hedda Gabler*, finally arrived. The play was scheduled to open the week before the week before Thanksgiving break, before the final crush of tests and papers. On the academic calendar, once they reached Thanksgiving, the semester was all but over. Then, with only a couple of weeks before final exams, coursework could no longer be ignored.

Alan and Erica were there on opening night, as they were expected to be. No one could accuse Canfield of not giving its all to the theater program. For the setting, Ibsen describes a villa that the family could not afford, purchased by Tesman in the mistaken belief that this would please his wife. It was duly decked out. What had been a cluster of chairs in rehearsal was now a beautifully upholstered divan in a tasteful shade of robin's egg blue. Erica wondered how much use they would get out of this particular piece of furniture once the show had completed its run of five performances. They might find room in Henry Higgins' library in *My Fair Lady,* or in one of the elegantly appointed drawing rooms of *The Importance of Being Earnest*, where the characters sipped tea and lobbed grenades disguised as *bon mots*. For now, it made a notable accent piece in the humdrum life that Hedda yearned to escape.

Even the divan could not distract attention from the acting onstage, which was the reason they were there in the first place. Alexis Grinnell was not the great beauty of her group, her medium brown hair and medium brown eyes finding stiff competition in Ashley Kwan's shock of blonde hair and Asian American ancestry, and Ava Levitan's auburn curls. Yet Alexis had whatever "it" is, that ability to make all eyes travel to her when she walked onstage. This was not achieved through outrageous behavior intended to get the audience's attention. She succeeded by staying in the moment and playing Hedda as written. Most of the cast were able to keep up with her, but, as the title of the play suggests, it was her show.

Much had gone into the making of this production, up to and including the death of one cast member. This score, even if settled, could never be made right. Looking at the play itself, as she did on this particular night, Erica had to admit that they had done a fine job.

"They were pretty good," she said to Alan as they left the theater on their way to the cast party at which they were also expected to put in an appearance. The school sanctioned one cast party, given in a reception room set aside for such functions. An after-party was rumored to follow in a location to be named later, most likely at the apartment of an upperclassman whose seniority enabled him or her to escape the dorms. Faculty would appear there too, but not in any official capacity.

"High praise, indeed," said Alan, "coming from you."

"No, really, I mean it. The acting was impressive. Alexis especially. Hedda Gabler is a tough to nut to crack. Given that she ruins lives, including her own, it's hard to make her sympathetic. You don't want to make her too much of a villain because then you lose the fact that she's a human being trapped in circumstances not entirely of her own making. The good old nineteenth century world with its strict rules for women."

"And for men," Alan reminded her. "It was no picnic for anyone, especially if your reputation suffered a hit. Then you were done in that society."

"Which Eilert Lovberg seems to want more than anything else," Erica said.

"I think he would like his manuscript back more than anything else," Alan offered.

"Too bad Hedda burns it."

"Not her best moment," Alan agreed.

"I will say that Kellan's Eilert held his own against Alexis' Hedda," Erica admitted.

"That's good of you," Alan replied. "Very generous. What have you got against him?"

"Nothing definite," she answered. "Just a feeling. He keeps popping up in the most unexpected places. Like our doorstep, on day one. Like the apiary, with a group of students that he has trained, whether through cajoling or threats, to recite Shakespeare with a background of buzzing bees."

"A man of many interests," Alan said. "So what?"

"His social life is equally interesting," Erica went on. "He seems to be with Alexis but is definitely seeing Ashley on the side, whom he calls Baby Cakes, if you can believe it. Ava, on the other hand, would appear to hate him."

"That's his complication, to be worked out among the ladies and himself. Definitely not part of my job description."

"I'm not saying it is," Erica insisted. "They can sort out their own tangle, which may be sorted out for them once they graduate. If they make it that far—"

"What do you mean by that?" Alan asked.

"Nothing ominous," Erica replied. "Kellan is two-timing the queen bee, and might be three-timing her if Ava were at all interested. So does Alexis' ignorance last until next May, if she is, in fact, unaware of what's going on? And if she knows, why put up with it? There must be a number of drones in the hive who would be only happy to serve the queen of the queen bees."

"I will definitely let them work that one out," Alan said. "Keep me posted." Returning to their original topic, he asked, "What did you think of Jordan's performance as Judge Brack?"

"Better than what I saw at rehearsal a few weeks ago. Not really in the same league with this Hedda and Eilert, but basically okay. Speaking of the judge, do you remember that production we saw Off Broadway a while back, when Judge Brack poured a can of soup over Hedda to show his power over her?"

"Yes," Alan said. "Tomato soup, the universal symbol of domination."

"That poor Hedda. To be doused eight times a week."

"Luckily, intermission followed," Erica said. "And she had a chance to hose down before the last act, which ends with a bang. The gun that's waved around in Act One—"

"Goes off in Act Two. A gunshot she directs at herself."

"Using her daddy's pistol."

"All in all, a fun evening," Alan finished. "Shall we go in?"

They had reached the reception room, which was already filled with enthusiastic theatergoers. Food had been laid out on long banquet tables, offering the type of fare that the school's catering service knew students would enjoy. Sandwiches, both meat bearing and not, on a variety of breads, rolls, and wraps led the menu, with desserts to follow, usually in the form of cookies and brownies that could be eaten without the use of utensils that could go missing. Nothing alcoholic was available in the beverage department, with only soda, water, and lemonade on offer for now. The students would rectify that later at a more discrete location. But free food was free food, and they tucked into the feast with gusto, severely diminishing the reserves before the actors had taken off their makeup, put on their party clothes, and made their way to the reception in their honor. When the cast finally entered the room, they were cheered between the last mouthfuls of food.

"Party at Kellan's in half an hour" was being whispered, stage whispered so everyone could hear, almost as soon as the cast arrived.

While Alan tried to scavenge some food for them, Erica caught a glimpse of Tasha across the crowded room, who waved before being swallowed by the crowd. They would have to compare notes later. Erica noticed that Luke, the play's director, had arrived with his leading lady. She saw him tilt his head toward her to catch something Alexis was saying. The decibel level in the room still allowed for conversation to be possible without having to yell. Alexis' proximity to his ear seemed unnecessarily close, especially when he turned his head to face her. They found themselves nose to nose, or more precisely, perfectly placed for a kiss on the lips. Luke was leaning in, and not in a good way.

Erica remembered the speech that Cressida had given at the time of Jessa Craven's death, when she described "a certain closeness within the theater community." Erica was pretty sure that this was not what Cressida had in mind. Surprisingly, the department's chair was nowhere to be seen this evening, so there was no way to know for sure. Erica could see why Kellan's cheating might not bother Alexis. She was out for bigger game.

When the news reached Erica and Alan about Kellan's party, the two chose to pass. Alan had already done his professional duty by congratulating everyone who deserved it and commending the rest with somewhat more muted praise, which they accepted with sincere thanks. Anyone he missed would receive his or her due in class next week. Erica, on the other hand, had already seen enough, and would need the weekend to regroup before facing them again on Monday.

As they walked back to faculty housing, Erica looked around to see if they were alone on the sidewalk. Seeing no one in their vicinity, especially anyone from the Theater Department, Erica turned to Alan.

"I thought you said that one reason Cressida and Luke were not a couple is because Luke is gay."

"In so many words, yes." Alan replied.

"You might want to reconsider. He's more open to experience than you might think. Or possibly, as we are all supposed to think." Erica described for Alan what she had observed between the director and his star.

"That was only one moment, Erica. It proves nothing."

"They were very close and they looked very close," Erica insisted.

"Show me," Alan replied.

"Gladly."

They stopped on the sidewalk and Erica issued a few instructions.

"You look straight ahead while I try to whisper in your ear. Then turn your head towards me."

Experienced at taking direction, Alan did as he was told, then added something of his own. The nearness of Erica made it easy for him to plant a kiss on her lips.

"Is this what you had in mind?" he asked.

"Exactly," she said. "Although I think we should try it again. Just to prove my point."

"You got it," he agreed and willingly complied.

Chapter 27

. . . birds do it, bees do it
Even educated fleas do it
Let's do it, let's fall in love.
Cole Porter

The performances ended over the weekend, but the
hoopla continued. The student paper, *The Canfield
Chronicle*, served up a glowing review. For the most
part, it was deserved. Attention was paid to each
member of the cast, all mentioned by name, including
the student who played the maid, Berthe.
Acknowledged only in passing was Luke Barton.
Apparently, everything on stage magically happened,
and the director's job was simply to keep the actors
from bumping into each other and that divan. Erica
doubted that Luke lived for good reviews in the student
newspaper, but he deserved more than a quick nod for
his efforts. The only review that mattered was the one
from his boss. Erica assumed it would be a rave. Then
again, after what had transpired at the cast party, maybe
not. Luke's extra-curriculars might not go down well
with Cressida for any number of good reasons,
including the rule about socializing with students. It
basically said, *don't*. Faculty fraternization seemed to
be okay with everybody.

Erica found Tasha in their favorite coffee shop on
Monday, this time without Daphne, who had been
called to the apiary at the last minute. They bought their
coffee and took a table at the back, away from the
students who preferred to be front and center, in order

to share all the news, fake or real, about what had happened the preceding weekend.

"I'm sorry we couldn't talk at the cast party," Tasha began. "I didn't expect such a crush."

"I have a feeling that many of the students in attendance were not taking theater courses, and may not have been in the opening night audience," Erica countered.

"I wondered about that," Tasha replied. "Is there a calendar somewhere that lists all the receptions that students can attend without anyone questioning their reason for being there?"

"Probably," said Erica. "They've figured out everything else about this place. At least they're out and about. Much better than sitting alone in their room."

"Yes," said Tasha. "Better to come to the cabaret. At least until the buffet runs out."

"What did you think about the show?" Erica asked.

"For a student production, I thought it was well done," Tasha began.

"Is that faint praise?" Erica asked.

"Not at all," Tasha answered. "The cast is always going to be a little uneven. Most of them were fine, with Alexis the best, and Kellan following after her."

"As he always does," Erica said.

"Well, almost always," Tasha said. "Did you go to the cast party after the reception?"

"No," said Erica. "You did?"

"I did," Tasha said. "I wanted to give it a look. I didn't last long."

"But long enough?"

"It was pretty lively, and a good time was being had by all. Maybe too good a time. There were only a few faculty sprinkled in, most notably—"

"Luke," Erica interjected.

"Yes, surprisingly. How did you know?"

"I saw him at the reception. With Alexis," Erica said.

"Yes," Tasha said, more emphatically. "Didn't see that one coming."

"How friendly were they?"

"They didn't cross any lines, at least not in public," Tasha admitted. "When I left, they were dancing the night away, but so was everyone else. Those two were definitely chummier than director and actor, especially when one of them is a faculty member. Not exactly the way the director and his leading lady should be celebrating the opening night of a student production."

"They did seem to be near to crossing a line at the reception," Erica interjected.

"And I didn't think he was interested in women," Tasha added. "I definitely didn't think he was interested in students."

"Who did? I wonder if this was entirely his doing. Alexis may be trying to prove a point," Erica said.

"What point would that be?"

"Proving she can get anyone she wants. If you have the director as your date—"

"That would be the same director who didn't cast her the first time around?" Tasha asked.

"Yes, one and the same. She got the part in the end, so, I guess, all is forgiven," Erica finished.

"That would certainly be a coup. Who is she proving this to?" Tasha asked.

"It seems that her boy Kellan has interests elsewhere." Erica described to Tasha the *ménage à trois* she'd seen playing out at various locations across campus.

"And it was right in his face," Tasha said. "At the cast party at *his* apartment. I do wonder if those two and that whole social set will hold together for the rest of the year," she mused.

"They made it this far," Erica replied. "I guess we'll see. And just out of curiosity," she continued. "What is Kellan's apartment like?"

"Nice," said Tasha. "Very nice. A one bedroom on the cushier side of town. Much nicer than my studio apartment with the Murphy bed that I have yet to come to terms with. That contraption was not manufactured in this century, possibly not in the last. When Sky comes to visit—"

"Sky is your significant other?" Erica asked. She knew of the existence of someone in Tasha's life, but nothing more.

"Yes, Sky has a three-year appointment at a college in Illinois. When I got a tenure track position at Canfield, it was too good to pass up. So we're enduring a commuter marriage. Even though Sky and I aren't married. Yet."

"I went through something similar a few years ago," Erica said. "Alan was performing in London, a production of *Othello* that transferred from New York. I got a teaching job at Brixton, a few hours north of here, right after I finished my Ph.D. It was an emergency appointment. One year."

Erica chose not to include the fact that she'd been asked to stay on at Brixton University and didn't take up them up on their offer, or any of the offers made to her while she was there. The rigors of steady employment in academia being a given, Tasha didn't pursue that line of inquiry. She returned to safer topics.

"Sky and I get together when we can. We both have to travel to a major city to fly out of, so we take turns."

"And Sky is short for Skylar?"

"That's right," said Tasha.

The name was open to interpretation, and Erica was not ready to commit.

"And Skylar's field is?"

"She specializes in the history of Latin America."

Got it, thought Erica but said, "That's certainly a growing field."

"We've been together since graduate school," Tasha said. Erica knew that graduate school ended for Tasha just last year, and chose not to ask how long the two had actually been together.

"Sky's hoping that her appointment turns into something tenure track. I'm hoping she finds something tenure track a little closer to here."

"We can dream, can't we?" said Erica. "It's kind of nice to live with your significant other. At the same time, I'm still getting used to it."

"Aren't we all?" agreed Tasha.

"But back to the production," said Erica, making an abrupt shift in the conversation, which Tasha didn't seem to mind.

As the two quietly discussed the pluses and minuses of the performance they'd seen, another conversation was unfolding at the front of the coffee shop. Alexis, Ashley, and Ava had arrived. If there had been waves, these would have parted. Alexis accepted the praise of her peers with surprising grace. She could act in life as well as on the stage.

After ordering their coffee, the trio chose a center table and seated themselves before restarting the conversation that had already begun.

"They're joined at the hip from what I can see," said Alexis.

"She doesn't let him out of her sight," Ashley agreed.

"Would you?" Ava asked.

Everyone in the coffee shop could hear this conversation including Erica and Tasha at their secluded table in the back. Erica's first thought was that they were talking about Luke and Cressida, a place where Alexis had already interposed herself. Cressida's absence from the opening night festivities had yet to be explained, although it did provide Alexis with an opening. Why she pursued Luke remained a question, which Ava asked.

"Why did you—" Ava began.

"Why did I what?" Alexis replied sharply.

"Why Luke, of all people? I mean, do I need to state the obvious?" Ava asked, unfazed by Alexis' abrupt reply.

"You never need to state the obvious, not to me," Alexis said pointedly. "We know each other way too well for that. Why Luke? Because he was there. And *he* wasn't."

"He was there," offered Ashley helpfully. "They didn't come to Kellan's party. They ducked out early."

"See what I mean?" said Alexis. "A short leash."

Erica was quickly beginning to understand that Alexis' dream date resided closer to home—her home. Tasha had come to the same conclusion.

"Now that would be a coup," she whispered to Erica.

"Over my dead body," Erica replied.

"Don't tempt her," Tasha said.

Erica was debating whether this would be the ideal time to reveal herself and leave the coffee shop, when the decision was made for her.

"Let's blow this pop stand," Alexis quickly announced. "I don't want to be late for Advanced Acting."

"I'm sure you don't," Ava replied, while Ashley simply did as she was told. The trio rose as one, gathered their belongings, and left. Erica and Tasha departed soon after, to far less notice by the students who remained.

After class, Erica found Alan to let him know that he was reaching at least one student in a way he hadn't planned. Erica found the infatuation, if infatuation it was, to be amusing. Alan did not.

Chapter 28

Ah, pray make no mistake, we are not shy;
We're very wide awake, the moon and I!
W.S. Gilbert

It all began with Cressida's headache.

Cressida's excuse for missing the opening night of
the fall production was, as she later explained to one
and all, a terrible migraine. No one remembered her
ever having been bothered by headaches. Some thought
that the headache was Alexis, given her behavior
towards Luke, and his towards her, at the reception and
cast party. On both a personal and a professional level,
this was not the done thing. If Luke wanted to put his
career in jeopardy, he was free to do so. The question
remained as to why he would risk it.

Cressida would persevere and attend the remaining
performances, after what must have been a severe
talking-to about Luke's behavior on opening night. The
boat seemed to have righted itself by the next evening,
when Cressida appeared at the performance with Luke
in tow. Things did not end there, however. Cressida was
called in a second time by the police for more
background on students who knew Jessa Craven and
might provide useful information, in a search for names
that might not have come up previously. Cressida, who
was just trying to be helpful, had a name on her lips
almost before the question was asked: Alexis Grinnell.
"Had they talked to her?" she asked, giving them a brief
rundown on the casting process for the production of
Hedda Gabler.

They had not. The immediate beneficiary of Jessa's departure from the cast would be a logical person to call in. Apparently, the police force didn't put as much stock in gossip as the theater community did. Actually killing for a part was not within their usual range of motives, although people had certainly killed for less. Murder by bee sting was also a new one. Neither Jessa nor Alexis, for that matter, went anywhere near the apiary, so their names were not found on the current list of beekeepers. The police did follow Cressida's lead and called in Alexis for a chat, which she recounted to her friends as they waited for acting class to begin. With Alan's permission, Erica was sitting in that day, and slid unnoticed into the back row as the conversation began. She wanted to see Alan in action and got more theatrics than expected.

"Are they going to question all of us?" Ashley asked in a tremulous voice.

"Why would they question you? It's not your part she stole," Alexis haughtily replied. The police interview had become a badge of honor, her due and long overdue, at least in her estimation.

"What did they ask?" Ashley nervously inquired.

"They wanted to know how well I knew her. How I *felt* about her."

"What did you say?"

"I said that I didn't really know her and had no feelings about her. Why would I? I'm a senior and she was a sophomore. We wouldn't have much to do with each other."

"Well, you *were* in the same class," Ava said. "This one. She *was* in Advanced Acting."

"Oh, right," Alexis replied, as if the thought were just occurring to her. "They might have mentioned that. But still, I didn't *know* her."

"I did," said Kellan, surprising the rest of his entourage and most of the class, who were listening in as they scanned their phones. "I talked to her a little the day we were auditioning for *Hedda*."

"Did you give her any pointers?" Alexis asked archly.

"Why don't you rush right over and tell them that?" Ava suggested. "I'm sure they'd be interested. Or have they called you in already?"

"Not yet," Kellan replied, with acid in his voice, directed toward Ava. "And I plan to keep it that way."

"You do that," Alexis said, while Ashley remained silent.

Luckily, Alan chose this moment to enter the theater, ending the conversation. He nodded to Erica seated in the last row of the theater, who nodded back. The rest of the class turned to see her, unaware of her presence until now. Ava Levitan grinned at her, while Alexis Grinnell blushed a vivid shade of crimson, which surprised Erica, who'd been impressed by the student's usual composure. When she made Alan aware of Alexis' more than academic interest in her instructor, this had impressed him not at all. He ran the class as business as usual.

"So, remind me, who are we going to hear from today?" Alan asked, as two students rose to prepare for the scene they were presenting. "And put your phones away before they begin," he said.

As the scene began, Erica sat up straighter in her seat to get a better view of the events unfolding onstage. Alexis, on the other hand, seemed to sink into hers.

Chapter 29

That's what friends are for.
Burt Bacharach and Carole Bayer Sager

One of the many curious customs in the Theater Department at Canfield was to hold auditions before the end of the fall semester for the two major productions in the spring. This might give the musical a running start when the spring semester began, since it was first on the schedule. It didn't really explain why the cast for the second play, which would not be performed until later in the spring, had to be decided before Christmas. Perhaps it was for the sake of convenience. When the results were posted on the bulletin board outside the Brink, dreams could be crushed or schedules altered, giving students ample time to make the necessary adjustments.

Erica strode with purpose across the campus, not so much because she had places to go and people to see, but because the weather had turned nippy. As she passed the bench at the center of the quad, she was surprised to see anyone seated there. The occupant was leaning forward, her elbows resting on her knees, muttering to herself. Usually, Erica would have left her alone to bemoan her fate, or possibly a recent break up. As she neared the bench, Erica realized that she knew the student sitting there. It was Ava, who, surprisingly, was alone, out of the sight and supervision of her friends. Erica's destination was the library, which would still be there when she arrived.

Ava looked up as Erica said, "We've got to stop meeting like this," choosing not to mention the tears that were running down the student's face.

"Oh, hi, Professor Duncan," Ava said, quickly rubbing away the evidence of her distress. A thorough wipe of her cheeks left smeared mascara as the only clue.

"Are you okay?" Erica asked, trying to keep her tone neutral and treating this, as much as possible, as a normal conversation.

"Yes, fine, thank you," Ava replied, the picture of politeness, her training kicking in along with a demonstration of her resolve. Not for nothing was she viewed as one of the top acting students in the department. Erica wondered what had caused these tears, specifically, if the cast list has been posted and things had not gone as expected. When this happened in the fall, the consequences were severe. Whether the events of the fall were connected to the death of Jenna Craven had yet to be determined. People in official and unofficial capacities were still asking questions.

Erica had a few of her own.

"Did something happen? Was it something about the cast list?"

Ava looked as if Erica claiming that the world was flat would make more sense.

"No," Ava replied. "Nothing like that. I told you I was going to get Lady Bracknell. I did."

"Congratulations," Erica said. "Now that's official. Then, if you don't mind my asking, what's wrong?"

Ava looked away before she began speaking. "Nothing....Everything. I got the part I wanted. I should be happy."

Erica listened and said nothing, waiting for her to go on. Finally, she did.

"My friends have been my friends since I got here. We did everything together. Almost everything," she said, correcting herself.

Erica nodded, as if she understood more than she did.

"If I disagree with my friends, they will dump me," Ava admitted sadly. "And if they dump me, no one will have anything to do with me. Not much of a way to spend your last semester," she said, looking straight at Erica.

"Well, no," Erica said, agreeing with her. "Are you sure that things are one way or the other?" Aware that people in their early twenties tended to paint in broad strokes, she asked, "Is it all or nothing?"

"Oh, yes," said Ava. "They might tolerate a difference of opinion on something small, but when it comes to big things—"

"What things?" Erica wanted to ask but chose to bide her time, saying instead, "That's a pretty strict crowd you run with."

"They can be. I mean, they're great people; they always were."

Erica noted the use of the past tense in Ava's answer, as well as the forced enthusiasm that went with it, as if the student were trying to convince herself.

"I just have to decide what I'm going to do," Ava said, with a faltering resolve.

Erica continued to nod. "I don't know if this helps at all," she said, "but it's the type of question people have to ask themselves, often at your age. 'Who am I going to be? How am I going to make my way in the world?' Not only how will I make a living, but what kind of person am I going to be? It's a gradual process. The light doesn't go on one day, and you say 'aha,' and the decision is made."

"I thought I could at least get through college without having to deal with it," Ava answered ruefully. "But things have happened so fast, and now I—"

Before Ava could finish her thought, she was interrupted by someone calling to her from across the quad. "Hey, Avy. Avy," could be heard as a tall figure moved quickly toward them. Ava stopped speaking as Kellan had made his way to the bench.

"Avy?" whispered Erica to her young companion before he reached them. "Does it mean something?" she asked.

"It means that as far as Kellan's concerned, I'm a member of AV, short for the Audio Visual Club," Ava explained. "As in, you're a nerd."

"Oh," said Erica, as neutrally as she could. "What is Alexis' nickname?"

"Nymph? Goddess? Divine?" answered Ava.

I get the picture, thought Erica, but said instead, "And Ashley?"

"Don't ask," Ava answered. Erica remembered that Kellan's term of endearment for Ashley was "Baby Cakes." Most fitting as things had turned out.

"We were all looking for you," Kellan said as he approached them. "Congrats on getting the part. Want to get some lunch?" he asked with more urgency than the question seemed to require.

Ava looked as though eating would be the last thing on her mind, but she made no argument and began to pick up her things. As she did, Kellan said, "Hi, Professor Duncan. Fancy meeting you here. Again."

Erica icily replied, "Yes, Kellan, I'm thinking of holding my office hours here, on this very bench. At least until it snows. Feel free to stop by anytime."

Kellan offered a weak smile but no response as he waited for Ava. Before they departed, Ava turned to Erica and simply said, "Thanks for listening."

"Any time, Ava. You know that."

Ava nodded. She also had parting words for Kellan.

"Let's be clear, Kellan. My name is Ava. Not Avy. Even you can remember that," she said with a renewed firmness in her voice.

Well, at least one thing has been decided, thought Erica, who rose from the bench and walked in an opposite direction.

Chapter 30

Speak of me as I am . . .
William Shakespeare

Erica chose a table in an obscure corner on the top floor of the library to grade papers. She could have worked in her office, which offered privacy but a distinct lack of ambiance. For starters, her rigid office chair was not built for comfort. Erica hoped that she was not as inflexible with her students as that chair was on her lower back. So, to the library she went, thinking that interruptions would be kept to a minimum. Even during crunch times, students preferred to sit at the computers on the first floor, the better to meet and greet their friends while checking their online accounts, and, occasionally, studying. The idea of a flat wooden table unadorned by technology as a place to get work done was alien to most of them.

Erica sat hunched over the task before her, reading and commenting on papers. She had taught these students long enough to know where to look for the most promising answers and had started with these. The hard part of grading was not finding the top or the bottom of the curve. Those papers were easy to grade. The hard part was slogging through the vast middle, through the subtle distinctions that would make all the difference between a B-, a C+, or the rest of the grades all the way down the line.

At first, she was too preoccupied to notice the figure looming over her. Kellan was tall but seemed taller as he stood there, waiting for her to look up. His silence might be seen as overly polite in not wanting to interrupt her work. The effect was definitely creepy, which, on balance, may have been his intent. Erica knew that Kellan had friends everywhere. Still, she wondered how he had found her. Was there a symbol, similar to the bat signal but more likely a bee signal, that could light up the sky? An entire network of beekeepers to do his bidding—that would be an impressive achievement. Perhaps not all hives were ruled by a queen.

Finally acknowledging his presence, all she offered was a nonplussed "Yes?" Erica followed this up with "Is there something you want, Kellan?" Her attention was the obvious answer. He chose instead to answer a question with a question.

"I came over here to study," he began, in the tone of a servile freshman rather than the confident senior that he was.

Unlikely, from what I've heard, Erica thought while maintaining her pose of mild interest.

"Then I saw you here. Sorry to disturb your work. I just wondered, are you happy here at Canfield?"

Since neither the Theater Department nor any member of the administration felt it incumbent upon them to ask this question, Erica was stumped as to why Kellan thought he should jump into the breach. Erica was a member of the adjunct faculty and well aware of the status of part-timers at Canfield—they had none—which would include someone like herself, who had come as part of the package with their better known better half. The line of questioning opened up by Kellan was equally solicitous and presumptuous. Then again, she wanted to hear what Kellan had to say, the *why* of any scheme usually more interesting than the scheme itself.

"I'm fine, Kellan," she said. "Is there anything else?"

"Well," he replied, seating himself in an empty chair at the table without being invited. "The school cares a lot about whether students are happy with their professors. I think they should consider how happy the professors are. My dad says that Ph.D.'s are a dime a dozen. I don't know about that. I think it matters which Ph.D.'s, you know?"

"What does your father do, Kellan?" Erica inquired. It was a question she would never have asked if he had not introduced the subject.

"He's in business," was all that Kellan would say.

"Unhuh," Erica replied. "So, your point?" she asked, taking a not-so-subtle look at her watch.

"I'm not sure I have one," he answered. "I just wanted to make sure that everyone is happy at the place they're in. I'm sure your students are," he added, as unctuously as he could. "And if you are too. You do know that the students fill out online evaluations at the end of the semester?"

"I do know that."

"And the professor's behavior both in and out of class is taken into consideration when decisions are made for re-appointment."

"I am aware of that too," she said. "This is not my first teaching job."

Erica would not be seeking re-appointment for the spring, and Kellan would be not on that committee in any case. She could sense that he was coming to a point, though it was still unclear as to what that point might be. She decided to let him find his way there on his own.

"Well, it has been noticed," he said, making a sudden switch to the passive voice, "that you have been spending a lot of time with Ava Levitan."

Kellan let his words hang in the air for dramatic effect. This had no effect on Erica, who met them with her own silence. Having had only two conversations with Ava during the semester, both in public, both at the center of campus, there was nothing in her behavior that was in any way suspect. Something was troubling Ava, and Erica had yet to discover what it was. For the most part, Erica simply listened. Yet something about her proximity to Ava touched a nerve with Kellan, who seemed to think that Ava had revealed more to Erica than she actually had. Maybe it was just that Ava was turning to someone who was not in their immediate circle. Maybe Kellan simply wanted to keep tabs on her. Knowledge was power, and Kellan wasn't willing to sacrifice any of his, which became clear when he overstepped with his next comment.

"You know how people talk," Kellan said, the very model of discretion. "You wouldn't want it to look like things have gotten too personal."

"Why would anyone think that?" Erica asked sweetly.

"I'm not saying they do," Kellan answered. "But you certainly wouldn't want that type of thing to get around."

"What type of thing?" Erica asked, sounding her most innocent.

"Oh, you know. People can get the wrong idea sometimes. And it can move across campus so fast. Even if it's not true."

Exhibit A, as Erica well knew, was the whispering campaign that had transformed Joy from a pitied victim to a calculating villain almost overnight, a contradiction that had yet to be resolved. Kellan seemed to be threatening Erica with the same treatment, even though her stay at Canfield was almost over. Any suggestion of inappropriate attention toward a female student would be hard to reconcile with the fact that she arrived on campus with a significant other who was decidedly male. Kellan was going out on a limb with his implied threat to Erica's good name and reputation. His misplaced bravado made it clear that he felt threatened by something that Erica might know about him or the triumvirate that he served.

Erica decided that this conversation had gone on long enough.

"I wouldn't worry, Kellan," she said. "Sometimes the teller of the tale ends up with more problems that the person the tale is being told about. Especially on a small campus, like Canfield. It's not all that hard to root out the truth. If you know who to ask and where to look."

It was Erica's turn to let her words hang, and Kellan's just to sit there. Shortly thereafter, he hauled himself up from his seat. Raising himself to his full height, he looked down at Erica and offered these parting words, "We all care about Ava, and would hate to see anything happen to her." If he had screamed, "She's ours and you can't have her," it would have had the same effect. Erica looked up at him and said, "I'm sure you do," and returned to her work, choosing to ignore him as he walked away.

Kellan may have left, but the papers were still there. Erica hunkered down for one more go at them before giving up for the day. About five papers in, she looked up and saw that she had another visitor.

Either the bee signal was working overtime or a sensor had been secretly implanted on Erica, which gave her location at all the times. Tracking her cell phone wouldn't have worked because Erica's was frequently turned off, mostly because she never remembered to turn it back on. Sometimes, it was left at home. In any case, Daphne was approaching with a determined stride that she made no attend to disguise.

"Daphne, fancy meeting you here," said Erica, a little surprised to see a scientist in the section of the library usually haunted by those in the Humanities, given the volumes that surrounded them.

"Well, occasionally, they do let me out of the lab," said Daphne good-naturedly, though her tone belied her bearing. Daphne appeared to have something on her mind that she was about to share.

"Or the apiary," Erica said. "How are the bees these days?"

"They're fine," Daphne replied. "Getting ready for their period of hibernation," she added. This was clearly not the topic she had come to discuss.

Erica sat quietly, as she had with Kellan, letting Daphne find her own way to her point, which she quickly did.

"Speaking of the apiary," Daphne began, "I've been hearing some troubling things from a few of the students who work there."

"Really?" said Erica, genuinely surprised. "About what?"

"You, mostly," Daphne replied.

"Me? What have I done now?"

"It's no joke, Erica. I know you're here for a short time," she said, "but you never know. Something longer term could open up. You don't want to make any enemies while you're here."

From what Erica had seen of Canfield, one semester would do her just fine. Anything longer could definitely lead to problems. It wasn't that she was allergic to the country, to the leafy greenness of it all. Erica knew she needed to feel pavement under her feet to feel alive and truly at home. She chose not to mention this to Daphne, who soldiered on without waiting for any comment.

"Well, without naming names, one of the beekeepers, a *senior* beekeeper, in particular, has suggested to me that you have been giving him a hard time."

Erica could see that Daphne had no future in covert operations. She had already revealed that the student in question was a *he* and a *senior* beekeeper at that. Senior in beekeeping meant senior in class. Juniors had to wait until they were almost ready to graduate to assume that lofty title. Erica had met a few beekeepers in her time at Canfield, though not enough to field a quorum. This could be one and only one person. Erica wondered why Daphne was here pleading his case, and so soon after Kellan's own visit. Clearly, the beekeepers did not go in for subtlety.

"Is this a student in one of my classes?" Erica asked, knowing perfectly well that it wasn't.

"I don't think so," Daphne said. Not particularly practiced at this game, she looked uncertain as to how much to reveal. Erica could have saved her time and said the name. Instead, she wanted to see where this was going to get a better sense of why Daphne had initiated the conversation in the first place.

"So I'm giving a student whom I'm not teaching a hard time," Erica said. "Is there a specific area in which I have been remiss?" Erica asked primly, going all English teacher on poor Daphne.

"Just a general attitude was the impression I got," said Daphne.

"I see," Erica said, waiting for Daphne to go into more detail.

"This student has done so much for other students on campus," Daphne began. "He has real leadership qualities and brought a number of students into the beekeeping program. Most of them from the Theater Department. I'm sure you saw the performance with the

beekeepers   reciting   Shakespeare.   That   was
unforgettable."

Erica had been in attendance at that theatrical outing.
She was a little surprised to learn that Daphne had been
there too. While it had been staged at the apiary, the
whole thing seemed a little far afield for the busy
scientist. Daphne was such an upright citizen that Erica
thought it unlikely that Kellan had some type of hold
over her, either personal or professional. Erica assumed
that Daphne was just doing what she felt was right.
Why Daphne believed in the rightness of Kellan's cause
was another matter. Erica was reminded once again that
the bond between beekeepers should never be
underestimated. Still saying nothing, Erica broke her
silence only after Daphne's next comment.

"I would hate to see his last year at Canfield spoiled
after he has earned so much goodwill," she finished.

Erica took a breath before answering.

"Daphne, as you know, my appointment ends this
semester. There is no talk, nor do I expect there will be
any, of extending it. You're going to have to be specific
if there's something I've done that has shaken this
senior to the core. Did I insult his friends, his fashion
sense, what? I don't know that many students outside
my own classes. Very few of them are seniors. It's a
pretty small field to choose from."

In this lightly inhabited corner of the library, their
conversation, even *sotto voce*, had elicited some
shushes from their neighbors. Even if Daphne could not
quite get to the point, Erica was finished talking.
Daphne had one more thought to offer.

"Erica, remember to be kind. They're just kids," she
said.

Erica wanted to remind Daphne that one of these
"just kids" had died in a way that looked accidental but
was hardly unintentional. And one of these "just kids"

may have been the source of the bee if not of its sting. And a number of these "just kids" had motives that were less than pure. This was not the place and it would never be the time, especially if Daphne had drunk the beekeeper Kool-Aid, laced with honey and who knows what else, apparently served up by Kellan.

"I'll think about it" was all Erica could manage. Daphne, seemingly placated by her answer, turned and left, never having taken the seat that Erica failed to offer. Before anyone else made their way to her hiding place, Erica decided to leave too, following Daphne to the door while keeping a safe distance between them.

Chapter 31

Let me not to the marriage of true minds
Admit impediments. Love is not love
Which alters when it alteration finds,
Or bends with the remover to remove.
O no! it is an ever-fixed mark
That looks on tempests and is never shaken . . .
William Shakespeare

For one of the final assignments of the semester,
Alan had asked the advanced students to choose one of
Shakespeare's sonnets and turn the fourteen lines into a
scene, acting it instead of simply reciting it. This
sounded like an intriguing possibility to Erica, who
slipped quietly into the back row of the theater to watch
it unfold. It turned out to be time well spent.

Before things got interesting, however, she had to sit
through a number of unfortunate choices. The students
had not checked with each other beforehand, and
several had chosen Sonnet 116. Way too many
members of a class that numbered in the teens were
definitely not admitting impediments to the marriage of
true minds, whether acting drunk, sober, or in one case,
in a dreamlike state, better described as asleep. These
were not sweet dreams.

The three ladies held themselves until the end, the
self-appointed finale. They had consulted with each
other and come up with different offerings, beginning
with Ashley. She chose Sonnet 130, which begins, "My
mistress' eyes are nothing like the sun." The sonnet
sings the praises of a mistress who did not meet the

Renaissance ideal of beauty, whose voice is not like music, and whose tread is not light, airy, or goddess-like but distinctly heavy on the ground. And yet, as the speaker insists in the final lines, "by heaven, I think my love as rare/As any she belied with false compare." The choice itself was so unexpected that Ashley needed no unusual interpretation to dress it up, just a straightforward delivery of the lines, which she would have sung if she could. The scene was deemed a success by the class. When Ashley returned to her seat, she looked distinctly pleased, and rightly so.

Ava was up next, and her choice was not presented with the comic delivery that everyone expected from her. For some reason, she had selected Sonnet 71, which begins:

> No longer mourn for me when I am dead
> Than you shall hear the surly sullen bell
> Give warning to the world that I am fled
> From this vile world with vilest worms to dwell;
> Nay, if you read this line, remember not
> The hand that writ it; for I love you so,
> That I in your sweet thoughts would be forgot,
> If thinking on me then should make you woe.

"You sure she's the funny one?" Erica would ask Alan after class was dismissed.

To say that her audience was captivated would be an understatement. Ava seemed to be directing her speech to the section of the theater where her friends sat, though she took in the class as whole, including Erica, whom she spied in the last row. Like Ashley, she played it straight and showed herself to be completely in command of what she was saying. If the speaker might be read as someone contemplating suicide, Ava was the picture of someone who had no plans to harm herself. Her choice of sonnet seemed so unlike her that Erica wondered exactly who Ava was speaking to, or possibly speaking for. Perhaps it was someone who could no longer speak for herself, but whose message still needed to be heard. While listening to the sonnet, Erica thought it too bad that Joy was not there to see this for herself.

Alexis was the final presenter, presumably saving the very best for last. At first, she appeared to be going with the flow, dredging up Sonnet 116 one more time. If anyone's attention was flagging at the end of the class, and Erica's certainly was, Alexis' interpretation got them to sit up and take notice. Staring down her friends, she began the poem dripping with sarcasm as she intoned, "Let me not to the marriage of true minds admit impediment." The venom in her voice built from there. Her message was clear. Someone, or more than one someone, had betrayed someone else. Ava looked confused as her friend spoke, although Alexis' wrath did not seem to be directed at her. Kellan and Ashley, her actual targets, looked positively scared. Word had definitely reached Alexis that these two were friendlier than friends—her friends—had a right to be, and she was letting them know that in no uncertain terms. The message appeared to be received and understood.

"That was fun," Erica said to Alan when the class ended, and the students left to work out their détente. "What's on the syllabus for the next class? Mortal combat? Will you be bringing in a fight consultant?"

"A meditator would be a better choice," Alan said, lofting the strap of his bag over his shoulder. "One that works with twelve-year-olds, preferably. What do you think that was about?"

"Young love?" Erica said. "Trouble in paradise? I'm not really sure. I will say that Kellan *does* get around. I don't know what game he's playing, but Alexis is definitely not having it."

"And Ashley is?"

"For the time being, yes. The short time being, given that performance. It was more than a warning."

"And yet they all trotted off together," said Alan. "As if nothing was wrong."

"Well, they're keeping it among friends. In house, as it were, though I doubt anyone else would dare to go near them."

"Someone would want to?" asked Alan.

"True, they are a scary bunch. To everyone else and to each other."

"And how does Ava fit into all this?" Alan inquired as they walked out of the theater and headed for home.

"She does and she doesn't," Erica replied. "She can't stand Kellan, who seems to come with the territory. She knows her friends only too well, but they're her friends. With graduation looming, it's a little late in the game to find new ones."

"The devil you know—" Alan began before Erica interrupted.

"I hope not," she said.

Chapter 32

The jewels of our father, with washed eyes
Cordelia leaves you. I know you what you are,
And like a sister am most loath to call
Your faults as they are named.
William Shakespeare

There was a timid knock at Erica's office door as she sat contemplating the weekend ahead. The semester nearly ended, this would include piles of exams to grade. It was not the happiest of thoughts. She had left her door ajar, and it swung open before Erica had a chance to say hello. Before her stood Ava Levitan. The actress looked in desperate need of a script, but no one had any dialogue to offer, least of all Erica. All she could offer was a seat.

"Ava, come in," Erica said in her cheeriest tone. "Please, sit down," she added helpfully, pointing to a chair.

Ava did as instructed. If Erica had suggested that Ava recline on a bed of nails, the student would have done it and not felt the difference. The exhaustion on her face signaled that Ava had spent a sleepless night, and probably more than one.

"I'm glad that you stopped by," Erica continued. "It's way too cold to chat on that bench in the quad. But I'm always glad to see you. What can I do for you?" she asked offhandedly, as if Ava had stopped by to shoot the breeze.

Ava stared at a point across the room that did not include Erica in her line of sight. Erica could wait it out in the classroom for as long as it took students to come up with an answer, telling them that she found the silence relaxing. It remained to be seen how long this wait would be. Ava needed a nudge, and Erica could not serve as the prompter. The words had to come from Ava. While the student's anguish did appear to be genuine, she was known for giving truthful performances. Erica hoped that in this instance, the emphasis would be on the truth and not on the performance.

Ava took a deep breath and finally spoke.

"Professor Duncan, do you remember that day we talked about how you never really know what people are capable of, even people you think you know well?"

"I do," Erica said, remembering the event a little differently. At the time, Ava had done most of the talking. Even so, Erica nodded, which Ava seemed to find comforting as she continued.

"We—I mean, they—I mean, well, um, something happened on campus, and after that, there was a pretty big disagreement between me and my friends."

Erica didn't ask which friends because that would sound insincere. She did wonder how far that circle extended, specifically, if it went as far as Kellan, whom Ava barely tolerated, presumably for the sake of harmony in the group. Usually, the biggest *something* in Ava's world was when a cast list was finalized and posted outside the theater. Casting had gone like clockwork this semester—with one notable exception. In Ava's crowd, the choosing of Jessa Craven over Alexis Grinnell probably held more weight than the subsequent death of Jessa Craven. Erica expected that Ava's distress had more to do with the latter than the former, although the two seemed to be inextricably mixed.

Erica, on the other hand, lived in a different world where the death of a student would take precedence. She decided it was time to wade into this conversation, if only to get her toes wet.

"A lot of things happened on campus this semester," Erica began. "It would help if you could narrow it down to one."

"You know which one," Ava replied, now looking at Erica with an unwavering gaze.

"I guess I do," said Erica, sounding more tentative than she felt.

"It was horrible what happened," Ava began. "She was so young....It could have been any of us...."

Ava's voice trailed off. Erica feared that she was losing her. With Ava's train of thought visibly unravelling, Erica decided to reel things in.

"But it wasn't," Erica said. "First, you would need to have a severe bee allergy. Which, presumably, none of you do. Someone administered that bee to Jessa's leg, so someone would need a reason to do such a terrible thing."

Ava flinched at the mention of the girl's name, then asked, "Even if it was meant as a joke?"

"You're known for having a great comic sense, Ava. Which part did you find funny?"

"I don't mean a joke," Ava quickly answered. "If someone didn't mean things to turn out the way they did—"

"You mean just do harm as opposed to cause a death?" Erica asked. "Regardless of the reason, a girl died. It happened. What could possibly make this in any way okay?"

Ava had no answer. Erica was not sure how hard she could push, and in what direction, before Ava pushed herself out the door. She decided to take a different approach.

"Have you talked to anyone else about this?" Erica asked. "Your friends, for example?"

"All we do is talk," said Ava. "No, that's not true," she admitted. "Alexis talks, and we listen."

"And you don't always agree?" said Erica.

"Usually, we do," Ava replied. "Mainly because Ashley does whatever she's told. I may object, but I usually come around to Alexis' way of thinking."

"Because it's two against one?" asked Erica.

"Because it's too much trouble not to," Ava said. "And usually it's about nothing. Or nothing important. Really important," she added, more firmly.

"But this time it is," said Erica.

"I wouldn't be here if it wasn't," Ava said, as if this were obvious.

"And what about Kellan?" Erica asked. "Where does he stand in all this?"

"Kellan is no friend of mine," Ava replied sharply. "He's got plenty of friends," she continued. "He doesn't need me."

At least two good friends in this group alone, thought Erica. And this clarified the group dynamic as Erica had assumed it to be, at least from where Ava sat. It remained to be seen which issues the other three were debating. For the time being, Ava seemed to be the only one who was asking the questions.

"If I go against them . . ."

"I know, Ava, you've said that before. Maybe you need to be the one who's doing the talking, and they do the listening. And whether it's to one person or more, you need to tell someone what it is you know. There is a serious business. Whatever the truth is, whatever the consequences, you have to tell what you know about this."

"What if they blame me?" asked Ava. "I saw what they did to Joy Craven."

"Who blames you? For what?"

Ava was silent.

"You and your friends did a pretty good job of getting that rumor started."

When Ava opened her mouth to protest, Erica stopped her.

"I heard you. In the student center that day," Erica said firmly, which silenced any objection.

"I don't want to drag you into this," Ava began.

Not any further than I'm already in, thought Erica. She asked another question instead.

"Can you just walk away and say nothing? Graduate from Canfield and go on your merry way, to what, I have no doubt, will be a wonderful acting career? Or do you have to say something before you go, and tell the truth? To someone in authority, hopefully, or maybe even to me."

Erica let that idea sink in before continuing. "Ava, I can't be your moral compass. You have to do that for yourself. I guess it all depends on how you want to live your life. We talked about this on the bench that day, remember? About what kind of person you want to be. Can you live with yourself if you don't tell what you know? Can your friends?"

"I expect they can," said Ava quietly.

"Are you sure about that? You can be pretty convincing. Maybe you can bring them around," Erica said, wondering how many of their group were salvageable, or worth saving. Or simply not guilty, at least in the eyes of the law.

Ava chose this moment to get up from her chair.

"Thanks, Professor Duncan," she said. "You've helped a lot," she added, as if Erica had just gone over what to study for the final exam.

"I'm glad, Ava," Erica said hesitantly, unsure of what exactly she had done. "If there's anything else I can do—"

"Nope," the student replied in a tone that was almost spritely, in sharp contrast to the gloomy girl that had entered the office. "I'm good," she said as she made a hasty exit.

"Glad to hear it," Erica replied, startled by Ava's abrupt departure. Erica was not quite sure what had transpired here, though fairly certain that things were not as resolved as Ava's tone might suggest.

"Later," Ava said as she walked out the door.

Not that much later, as things turned out.

Chapter 33

Is there a murderer here? No. Yes, I am . . .
William Shakespeare

"Erica, may I speak with you?"

The chair of the Theater Department had poked her head out of the office as Erica passed her door, making it fortuitous timing for at least one of them. Erica was racing home after an extended stretch of grading.

"Of course, Cressida," she said, although her answer would be assumed by both.

"I need another faculty member to sit in on a meeting with some students in my office. *Now*," she said with subtle emphasis.

A little surprised that Luke had not been called into service, or that a lowly lecturer was deemed sufficient for the job, Erica simply nodded and followed Cressida to the inner chamber. While turning to reenter the office, Cressida added, "And you were around. As you so often are."

When Erica entered the room, she saw that Luke was, indeed, in attendance. As were three of everyone's favorite students: Alexis Grinnell, Ashley Kwan, and Ava Levitan. Alexis was trying to look unconcerned, while Ashley looked ill. Only Ava acknowledged Erica's arrival with a tiny smile that disappeared as soon as the conversation began.

"All right, ladies," Cressida said. "You may begin."

A few hours later, Erica dragged herself into the apartment and found Alan reclining on the sofa.

"They gave him up," she said.

"Who?" Alan replied, sipping a beer after a long day in the rehearsal room.

"The three queens. They gave up their drone. They went in and told what he had done."

"And what did he do?"

"Kellan was the one who injected the bee into the sleeping girl."

"What! Why in the world . . . ?" Alan sputtered.

"To please his lady, or ladies, fair," Erica said. "Or so he thought. So Alexis would get the part that she wanted. And he could lay it before her as a form of homage."

"He killed one student to get a part for another student? According to whom?"

"The news is all over campus," Erica said. "The students are abuzz with it—"

"Please don't," Alan began.

"Okay, sorry," Erica said. "The three of them went first to Theater Department, more specifically, to Cressida, who called in Luke to witness the conversation. And then me. Maybe to even the numbers. I happened to be walking by, lucky me. Anyway, it was Alexis in the lead when they reported him—"

"Isn't that her usual position?" asked Alan.

"Not on this one," Erica replied. "I had a pretty good idea that Ava was on board. Exactly how she got Alexis into that room I'll never know. Those two must have strong-armed little Ashley into the meeting. In any case, all three went."

"Sisters before misters," Alan said.

"Self-preservation before being charged as an accessory is more like it," Erica replied.

"Maybe."

"Anyway, after Cressida and Luke heard what the ladies had to say, they marched them over to the Security office, who called in the authorities. The three of them swore in unison that Kellan didn't intend to—kill her, I mean. But Jessa died, and he will be charged accordingly."

Erica waited for a moment, watching Alan absorb this information.

"Okay," he said. "Give me the details. I can see you're dying to."

"Maybe we should steer clear of the death references for the time being," she said. "Anyway, here it is.

"According to the ladies, Kellan pumped Joy for information while they were working together at the apiary—when Joy thought he was being *such* a good listener. Always on the lookout for new people to add to their number, Kellan wanted to know why Jessa wasn't a beekeeper too. Joy came up with the information that her sister had been stung as a child and was afraid of bees. Joy mistakenly thought that the previous sting might result in a slight sensitivity to bees but not a full blown allergic attack. Then Kellan did what he always did, and filed away this information for later use. As a *senior* beekeeper, he would know what the effect of another sting could be on someone with this type of sensitivity. But so far, it's all perfectly innocent because he did not act on this knowledge. And even Kellan could not foresee the casting of Jessa in a role coveted by Alexis. When the need arose, he acted, maybe not to eliminate the competition, only to sideline her, clearing the way for Alexis to get the part that she felt was rightly hers. Kellan wanted to put Jessa out of commission just long enough for Alexis to play the lead. The show must go on, and all that."

"So," Alan asked, "he just happened to have a bee handy?"

"No, not quite. That required some planning. Bees don't travel well, not unless they're in flight or in some type of protective packaging. The kind that protects both the bee and the beekeeper."

"Mostly the beekeeper, I would think," Alan interjected. "The bees can probably take care of themselves."

"I'm sure you're right," Erica said. "Did you know, if you want to start your own hive, you can purchase your own queen bee?"

"I thought I already had my own queen bee," Alan said.

"Of the apiary type," she replied. "They throw in a few 'attendant bees' because without them, she wouldn't survive. A lady's got to eat."

"She eats the other bees?" Alan asked.

"No," Erica said. "She needs the others to provide food for her because the queen cannot feed herself. She doesn't bite the hand that feeds her."

"Or she orders a lot of takeout," said Alan. Erica did not look amused.

"So, bees by mail," he said.

"Yes, you can order anything online. You can send away for a queen to start your very own hive."

"Now I know what to get you for Christmas," Alan said.

"Pass," Erica said. "Hard pass," she repeated. "But guess who knew that you can order bees by mail."

"Kellan?"

"Right again. Instead of extracting a queen from one of the hives on campus, he got himself a starter set through the mail. Maybe the Canfield queen would be missed? Anyway, he got a queen and a few attendants. These were Russian bees, not the type they use in the hives here. I remember Daphne saying that it was odd when the 'killer' bee was identified as Russian."

"No Russian bees because . . . ?"

"They don't play well with others," Erica answered. "Leave it at that."

"Okay," said Alan, uncertainly.

"Leaving Kellan to make that lonely walk across campus on the fateful night, bee in hand, or jar. I doubt that he would risk his pretty face and handle a bee without wearing the hat and veil for protection," Erica went on. "Not to mention the gloves. Beekeeping is not literally a hands-on experience, given all the protective gear. Even professional beekeepers wear the hat, although they sometimes work without gloves when checking the hives for honey."

"A hand full of bee stings would be a dead giveaway, or at least highly suspicious," offered Alan.

"Yes," Erica said. "And even Kellan would have a hard time carrying off the full hazmat suit. But a hat and gloves would fit under his arm, and no one is the wiser."

"Chalk it up to an interesting fashion choice," Alan said.

"Done," said Erica. "In any case, Kellan lives off campus, in someplace nice according to Tasha, who saw his apartment on opening night at the after-party. His buzzing package would not have to go through campus mail and catch anyone's attention. That type of special delivery tends to be overnighted anyway. As an advanced beekeeper, Kellan would be able to extract a bee and place it in a small glass jar, with air holes in the lid so it could survive the trip across campus. Kellan had heard about Jessa's plan for her performance piece—apparently, they discussed it as they waited to audition—so he knew exactly when she would make her return trip to the theater to catch a glimpse of the ghostly Rosaline. He waited for an hour late enough for Jessa to be caught napping and then snuck into the theater, having long ago 'borrowed' a key to the back entrance and made a copy of his own. Security at the theater being almost non-existent, and no doors closed to Kellan. The mystery of the missing supplies that Cressida mentioned at the beginning of the semester may have solved itself. Exactly what Kellan wanted with a few cans of paint or rolls of duct tape, we may never know. Maybe it was all about the stealing."

"Theft is the least of his worries," Alan said.

"That's for sure," Erica answered. "Anyway, the theater was dark when Kellan arrived, and Jessa appeared to be asleep, presumably having turned off the ghost light. By the light of his silvery cellphone, he crossed the stage. The bee was none too happy at this point, so Kellan had to remove the lid quickly, placing his hand, protected by his beekeeper glove, over the top of the open jar. He flipped over the jar and placed it on Jessa's leg, leaving the bee to do what bees do when they get angry or scared. It stung her. He quickly exited stage right, because, as we know, there is no exit stage left. He managed to smear any tracks he made upon entering, so there was bee pollen on the floor from the shoes he wears everywhere, including the apiary, but no clear foot prints. The pollen incriminated Joy at first, helped along by the whispering campaign staged by the three witches—I mean, the three queens—who apparently were not co-conspirators."

"Are you sure about that?"

"Let's remember who gave him up. In specific detail, repeating everything he told them, presumably in confidence. And, strangely enough, this has not turned into an exercise in finger pointing. Not yet, anyway. When Kellan was finally located, no doubt wandering the campus in search of his three ladies, he did not implicate them. Loyal to the last, I guess. I doubt he'd go down all by himself if he could prove that they were in any way involved."

"Probably true," Alan said. "What about the actual co-conspirator? The anonymous bee. Can I assume that it was a queen bee that did the deed?"

"No, you can't. Although a drone did do it. Not a drone from the bee family, but the drone, Kellan."

"Please explain," Alan said.

"Only female bees can sting—you go, girls—while the male bee, the drone, has no stinger. And while we're at it, the queen has a stinger but it's smooth, so she can sting more than once and live to tell the tale. The queen only stings the up-and-coming queens in the hive, before they reach their full maturity and can replace her. It had to be a worker bee, female, of course. The stingers of the worker bees are barbed. It goes in once and stays there. And that's all she wrote for the stinger, and for that particular bee."

"Ouch," said Alan, "but not entirely surprising. Leaving it to the workers, as usual."

"With a little help from their friend Kellan. It took a while, but he finally reported back to the ladies and told them what he'd done. Not right away, and not yesterday either. In terms of the calendar, I would guess that he held onto this information for weeks after it happened. I'd put the date he spilled the beans at a couple of weeks ago, when Ava, she of comedy fame, began to get very serious. She started talking about not really knowing her friends or what they were capable of."

"So they knew and didn't immediately run to the police, or even to Cressida?" Alan said.

"Yes, touching, isn't it? Again, loyalty, in a twisted kind of way."

"And no one's asking them why?" Alan wanted to know.

"Not yet."

"So their loyalty is the self-protective kind?"

"I don't know," Erica admitted. "One sticking point—sorry, too close to a bee reference—is that Jessa was found in a sitting position. Either she sat up suddenly, in a state of shock when the sting happened, or she was placed in that position, presumably by Kellan. This would move the dial from accidental to deliberate, from manslaughter to murder. Kellan insists that he never moved her. He, or possibly his lawyer, is adamant on that point. But it facilitated Jessa's death by allowing the venom that was toxic to her to race through her system."

"And it's not like they can dust for prints," Alan offered.

"Even if they could, he was wearing gloves."

"So, are these ladies in trouble for withholding information?" Alan asked. "Or possibly embroidering what they knew if the 'he didn't mean it' angle was their contribution to the narrative?"

"Not at the moment," Erica answered. "Probably not ever. One student in deep trouble may be enough for this campus to handle. Kellan expected to be thanked for his efforts, profusely, no doubt. They were willing to be served—and two of them serviced—by him. But singly or as a group, the three queens decided to draw the line when someone died and they could be implicated."

"It took them long enough to come to that conclusion," Alan said.

"Or maybe, with graduation only a semester away, they thought it could damage their careers," Erica replied.

"So, whether to protect themselves or stung by an attack of conscience, they served him up," he finished.

"I thought we were staying away from any talk of bees," she said.

"Sorry," he said sheepishly.

"It's unavoidable. They're all around us," Erica admitted. "And surprisingly, it was Alexis, not Ava, who led the troupe into Cressida's office. I guess a starring role is a starring role, whatever that might be. And apparently, the three of them can be very convincing."

"I told you they were good."

"This time they weren't acting. At least, I hope not. They were telling the truth."

"That can be convincing too," Alan said. "And what about Kellan?"

"In his defense, they insist that Kellan was only trying to incapacitate Jessa, not kill her. So, a prank gone terribly wrong. If they made that up or he did is still unclear. And at this point, Kellan isn't adding anything to his previous statement. Kellan's father is the CEO of a Fortune 500 company, and Kellan has been lawyered up to the top of his deeply confused head."

"So his daddy's rich. I wonder if they'll trot out the 'but he's from a good family' defense," Alan asked.

"Judges have lost their seats on the bench for buying that one. I expect they'll go for something less provocative," Erica answered.

"The girl is still dead," Alan said, who paused before asking, "And why did he feel he had to serve his queen bees, especially to this extent? He seems to have had plenty to fall back on. A rich daddy, to start with—"

"You should probably check with his mother on that. Who is undoubtedly good looking," Erica said.

"I expect she has more pressing matters on her mind," Alan said. "Like keeping her son out of jail. Let's save the drive-by psychology for another day."

"Gladly," said Erica. "Or leave it in the hands of the high-priced shrink who is being hired. Or already on the payroll."

"Done," said Alan.

"Yes," Erica continued, "Kellan will be taking next semester off. Not just to deal with his legal troubles. The college is not keen on having an alleged murderer in their midst, even if he insists that he really didn't mean it. They haven't chucked him out just yet. He's suspended, pending the outcome of the trial."

"The incident with the bee was not enough to get him expelled?"

"See above, Alan. His daddy's rich. And you never know. They might not want to be sued for assuming someone's guilty before it's proven beyond a reasonable doubt."

"And what about the apiary? Will it survive?"

"Strangely enough," Erica said, "there's no talk of closing it. Someone weaponized a bee. Apparently, the folks in charge don't see that as the bee's fault. The apiary is safe, for the time being."

"Working along the same lines as the argument that guns don't kill people—" Alan began.

"People do, right. I'm not arguing the merit of that argument," Erica said. "But if that kind of thinking keeps the bees on campus, fine with me."

"You've grown accustomed to their faces?" Alan asked.

"No, I still don't want them anywhere near me," she said. "Maybe after a semester at Canfield, I do have a better sense of why the bees are here, and why we need to keep them around. We would more than miss them if they were gone. No bees, no flowers, and then, there goes most of the world's food."

Erica waited for a moment, before adding, "There's one thing that does concern me."

"Only one?" Alan asked, but she let that go.

"If, in a few years' time, you run into any of these lovelies at an audition, may I strongly suggest that you run—quickly—in the opposite direction?"

"Way ahead of you on that one," he said.

Chapter 34

*How lucky I am to have something that makes saying goodbye
so hard.*
A.A. Milne

A slight figure entered the theater, through a door
that had deliberately been left open. The only
illumination was the work light at center stage, shining
a ghostly blue. It was enough, it would do. Moving
toward the stage, she took the flowers from her back
pack and unwrapped them, removing the cellophane
and then noisily crumpling it. She walked by the first
row of seats and stopped at the edge of the stage. She
did not climb the steps to mount the stage in which she
never had any interest. Reaching up, she laid the
flowers center stage. This might have been her sister's
opening night bouquet, if her sister had lived to see an
opening night.

As she placed the flowers, Joy felt a hand brush hers.
She stiffened for a moment. By order of Cressida
McPheers, no one was allowed in the theater this
evening, not even in the downstairs workshop where
the building of scenery never seemed to end. Yet Joy
felt the presence of someone there.

"Good bye, Jessa," she whispered.

Two onlookers, the only two who dared to ignore
Cressida's directive, stood by as Joy walked out of the
theater. She never looked back. For her, there was
nothing to see. She would be transferring to another
school, the one she had planned to attend until Jessa
insisted that they matriculate together. Joy would have

endured anything, even dressing alike for four years at Canfield, to have Jessa by her side. Sadly, her future would be hers and hers alone.

The spectators watched silently, waiting until Jessa closed the theater door behind her. The woman in nineteenth century dress looked from the door to the teenage girl by her side. Her companion wore sweat pants and a hoodie, twenty first century dress, suitable for daywear or for sleeping on a stage. The emotional weight being all on Joy's side, her sister looked down at the flowers, strangely unmoved by what she had witnessed. Rosaline seemed impatient to depart, perhaps with some ghostly duties awaiting them. At least she would now have some company. Jessa spoke first, remembering a line from the play she had finished the night before she died.

"'Lord, what fools these mortals be—'" she began.

"*Tell* me about it," Rosaline said, looking directly at her companion.

Without further comment, the two turned and walked stage left, where there was no exit, disappearing into the semi-darkness of the night.

Chapter 35

> *That is the question.*
> William Shakespeare

The next morning, the rental car was packed and ready for the trip home, the heat already churning inside for the ride back to the city. The sun was out and the roads were clear, with no sign of snow, if the local forecasters were to be believed. No one had appeared to help them pack the car, Kellan being otherwise engaged. Their grades submitted, their good byes said, they had little to say to each other. As they returned home, Alan was at the wheel with Erica staring out the passenger window at nothing in particular.

"Will you miss anyone?" he asked her after twenty minutes of riding in silence.

"I have Tasha's email address," she said, "and she has mine. We will email back and forth until we don't."

"Sounds like a plan," said Alan. "Anyone else? What about the little beekeeper boy you told me about?"

Erica thought for a moment. "You mean Trent? That seems unlikely. I'm glad he found a place to fit in, but Bee Strong seems to have taken over his life. If they start wearing armbands and singing anthems about how tomorrow belongs to them, there is genuine cause for concern."

"Not Daphne?" Alan asked.

"Not so much," Erica replied. "She's also pretty deep into the bees." *Or was it the beekeepers?* Erica wondered, remembering Daphne's robust praise of Kellan. She wondered what Daphne thought of him now.

"And you?" she asked sweetly. "Anyone you will miss?"

"Probably not," he said.

"I bet you're going to miss hanging out at the malt shoppe with the mean girls," Erica volunteered.

"There's nothing more dangerous than that, as Kellan could probably tell you, if he were allowed to say so. I'll wait and see if the professional winds blow any of us together," Alan replied.

"You think you're going to run into Luke at an audition? Or Kellan in a prison outreach program?" she asked.

"He's not convicted yet," he countered.

"Here's hoping," she said.

"I don't know what his plans are," Alan continued. "Luke's, I mean. We know what Kellan will be up to for the next few months, if not years. It would seem that Luke and Cressida have overcome their differences. He was back at his post, by her side, through all the turmoil at the end of the semester."

"True," said Erica. "It looked for a while as if he might be seeking greener pastures. Maybe he realized that this gig is about as green as it's going to get for him. Again, Cressida may have the last word on that."

"Maybe, maybe not," said Alan. "At this point, I expect his transgressions are a distant memory."

"Yes," said Erica. "So hard to get good help these days."

"I don't know. It's a tough job market. And sycophants aren't that hard to come by," Alan replied.

"True again. He may need to go into overdrive in the bootlicking department if he wants to keep his spot," Erica offered.

"Let's leave that up to him—and her," Alan said.

"Deal," said Erica.

"And for once, this is a mystery you didn't solve," Alan began.

"And all the better for it," Erica agreed. Fairly certain that she may have helped push things toward their eventual conclusion, Erica still felt that she had kept her promise to Alan, honored the spirit if not the letter of the law. She thought it best not to mention this to him, especially in a moving car. Better to wait until her feet were safely back on pavement.

"Speaking of next moves," Alan asked, "What do you think yours will be?"

"Good question. I hadn't really thought about it. Not enough to come up with a plan."

"No time like the present."

"What about you?" she asked, trying to change the subject.

"I hope to be gainfully employed in the theater," he answered.

"Sounds like a plan," Erica admitted. "Is it confirmed?"

"Still pending, but looks good," Alan said.

"Sounds promising," she said.

"Yes, it does. Now back to you."

"Honestly, you will know as soon as I do. I promise."

"I'll keep you to that," he said.

"I wouldn't have it any other way," she replied, before adding, "Speaking of overdrive."

"Yes?"

"I'd like to leave this adventure in the rear view mirror as quickly as possible. Can you move this thing any faster?"

"Your wish, my command," Alan said, pressing on the gas pedal to achieve a speed that would not catch the notice of the state police patrolling the highway.

"Many thanks," said Erica. She settled into her seat, eager for the journey ahead.

ABOUT THE AUTHOR

 Laura Shea is a professor of English at Iona College. She is the author of *A Moon for the Misbegotten on the American Stage*, and her essays and reviews have appeared in *The Eugene O'Neill Review*, *Theatre Journal*, *Theatre Annual*, *The Comparatist*, and *American Theater Web*. She has also worked in different professional capacities in theaters in Boston and New York. In addition to *Murder in the Wings*, she is also the author of *A Dying Fall*, a mystery novel set in academe, and *Murder at the People's Theater*. She lives in New York.

Made in the USA
Monee, IL
17 July 2020